"What are those?"

"Our alpacas."

His face puckered. He watched them grazing, seemingly disappointed with what he saw, yet too fascinated to look away. His slouched posture made her think of a child forced to endure the family vacation.

Under a frown, his eyes searched the grounds. "Aren't there any cows—or horses?"

What was wrong with this guy? Most people found alpacas charming. Perhaps her first instinct had been right, and he was a con artist after Hannie's property. A cattle or horse ranch might be easier to sell.

"No, just alpacas." With a wave, she said, "Oh, we do have some Angora rabbits."

He turned and glared at her. "Rabbits."

Suddenly feeling like a reprimanded child, she pointed weakly to the henhouse attached to the far side of the barn. "And chickens."

He shook his head just a fraction. "Alpacas, rabbits, and chickens."

Was that a snort? How dare he mock something into which Hannie and David had poured heart and soul.

Before she realized it, she placed her hand on her hip and gave him an indignant glare.

"I'm sorry. I expected. . ." His shoulders sagged. "This is all so surreal to me."

Ruthanne suddenly wished she knew more about this man's history. When had he and his mother become estranged? Why hadn't Hannie told her about him? And the question Ruthanne would rather not explore: What about the past had Hannie felt necessary to keep hidden?

KATHLEEN E. KOVACH and her husband, Jim, raised two sons while living the nomadic lifestyle for over twenty years in the Air Force. She's a grandmother, though much too young for that. Now firmly planted in Colorado, she's a member of American Christian Fiction Writers and leads a local writers group. Kathleen hopes her readers will giggle through her books while learning the spiritual truths God has placed there. Visit her Web site at www.kathleenekovach.com.

Books by Kathleen E. Kovach

HEARTSONG PRESENTS
HP717—Merely Players

Don't miss out on any of our super romances. Write to us at the following address for information on our newest releases and club information.

Heartsong Presents Readers' Service
PO Box 721
Uhrichsville, OH 44683

Or visit www.heartsongpresents.com

God Gave the Song

Kathleen E. Kovach

Heartsong Presents

I dedicate this book to my husband, Jim, who makes my heart hum every day.

I would also like to acknowledge the people who helped me research this story. To Stargazer Ranch in Loveland, Colorado, and owners Cynthia Fronk and John Heise, my extreme gratitude for walking me around your ranch, introducing me to your alpacas, and sharing your love of these unique creatures. And to the many people I met at the State of Jefferson Alpaca Show in Medford, Oregon, especially Gabrielle Menn, Janet Hedley, and Richard Smith.

I'd also like to thank my sister, Shari Warren, my mother, Ruth Keal, and my brother-in-law, Neil Warren, for setting aside their busy lives and becoming tour guides for a couple of weeks.

And finally, my critique partners who keep me grounded. To JOY Writers and ACFW Crit2, I thank all of you for going the extra mile and teaching me how to make it all work.

A note from the Author:
I love to hear from my readers! You may correspond with me by writing:

Kathleen E. Kovach
Author Relations
PO Box 721
Uhrichsville, OH 44683

ISBN 978-1-60260-590-9

GOD GAVE THE SONG

Our mission is to publish and distribute inspirational products offering exceptional value and biblical encouragement to the masses.

PRINTED IN THE U.S.A.

one

Ruthanne stood over Hannie in the hospital bed, wincing as the older woman rasped out another bone-jarring cough. Her employer and friend was still young at sixty-six, but her health had declined since the hospital admitted her a few days prior. It was only pneumonia. People—strong, faith-filled people like Hannie—recovered every day from that illness.

Why did she ask for her lawyer?

Hannie's nephew, Paul, entered with Vaughn Stanton. Paul gently slipped his hand into the once-strong palm that even now looked oddly ready to pitch hay. "Auntie, we're all here."

Hannie opened her eyes and removed the oxygen mask, keeping it near. Vaughn removed a small digital recorder from his pocket and turned it on.

With a thin voice that sounded like sandpaper on wet wood, Hannie spoke. "I have a son, and I want you to find him."

ða

A month later

Skye stood in the doorway, mere feet from his mother in the hospital bed. The *shush-poc* of the respirator accused him, as if it knew what he was thinking.

He should go to her, hold her hand. Let her know he was near. Pray for her. But who was he kidding? He wouldn't even have come if the lawyer hadn't been so insistent. Truthfully the only reason he agreed was to ask the woman one simple question.

Why?

"Excuse me."

Skye turned toward the male voice behind him.

"Do you know my aunt?"

"I'm her. . .son." Skye shook off the spiders of anxiety clinging to his flesh due to his mother's nearness and reached for the man's outstretched hand. "Skye Randall."

"Paul Godfrey, her nephew. Her lawyer told me he'd contacted you yesterday. Thank you for coming so soon."

Skye searched the younger man for a family resemblance. Paul's dark hair matched his own, but Paul's eyes were a deep brown while Skye's were blue.

"We're not related, are we?" Skye felt disjointed, like a puzzle not yet completed.

"Not by blood, no."

The stab of regret surprised Skye.

He glanced at the paper placard outside the door with his mother's name. HANNAH GODFREY. She must have married this man's uncle. He wanted to ask if his mother had other children but thought better of it. Would the answer be too much for him to bear?

Skye jerked his head toward the bed. "When can I talk to her?"

Paul looked toward the floor. "They didn't tell you her condition when you came in?"

"No. Mr. Stanton gave me the room number, so I found it on my own."

"Oh man." Paul's gaze darted down the corridor. "The doctor should be here soon. That's why I'm here." He rubbed the back of his neck. "You should know though. She's in a coma."

The four simple words carried the weight of a sucker punch.

The man moved to the side of the bed and lifted her hand. His fond gaze directed toward his aunt spoke volumes to Skye. "Aunt Hannie has a tendency to overdo, to the point of exhaustion sometimes. Add to that her visits to children's hospitals, nursing homes, prisons—she ended up contracting a virus that turned into pneumonia. But then it took a nasty turn."

The doctor entered, interrupting the list of saintly duties this woman had supposedly performed. He forced a brief smile to his lips as Paul introduced the doctor to him.

Dr. Harris lifted the chart at the end of the bed and made some notations. "Your mother has ARDS, Acute Respiratory Distress Syndrome. What this means is that the pneumonia is now in the tissue surrounding her lungs. This takes more time to heal since it's impossible to get medicine there. To make her more comfortable during the process, we chose to put her into a drug-induced coma this morning."

"Then she's not going to die?" Skye's words spilled out in an emotionless query. However, when Paul's head snapped up, he regretted being so blunt. *Sorry, Lord.*

The doctor placed his dark hand on Hannie's white wrist and inspected her fingers. "Ah, color is coming back." He gently laid her hand down and regarded Skye. "I'm not going to lie to you. This is a very serious illness. The survival rate is about 60 percent, but that's better than the 30 percent it's been in the past. We're more aware of the disease now, and we have better equipment." He patted Skye's shoulder on the way out. "Don't worry, we'll do everything we can to keep her in the right percentile."

Paul walked out behind him, shaking his head and muttering, "A 40 percent death rate."

What was he? A glass-is-half-empty kind of guy?

Skye tagged on to the end of the procession, not eager to be left alone with the stranger in the bed. Coma. He hadn't expected that. He'd wanted to get answers from the woman who turned her back on him, and now all he had was more questions. And a bit of guilt. This Paul guy really seemed to care about her, yet the woman he described was nothing like the one Skye had known. How was he supposed to reconcile the two?

Conviction slowly seeped into his soul. He hadn't communicated with God since the lawyer called him. He didn't want to pray about the situation. He only wanted to hear his mother's story. But things were getting complicated, so he managed to wring out three words: "God, be near."

They entered a waiting area with putty-colored faux leather couches and armchairs. A television droned on in the corner, with the morning news turned so low it was barely audible. Large, frameless paintings of flowers hung on each wall. The cheery yellows, greens, and reds only served to agitate Skye further, and he clenched and unclenched the car keys in his hand, making them jangle.

As they sat, Paul seemed to have trouble making eye contact. "This must be awkward for you."

"You have no idea."

"I'm sure Aunt Hannie regrets losing you."

Skye thrust himself from the chair. "She didn't lose me. She. . ."

. . .left me.

It took all his restraint not to throw his keys at the television. How much did this man know?

After an uncomfortable moment, Paul said, "Did he mention her property?"

"He said he wanted to meet with me tomorrow regarding it. What? Does she own a small plot of land?" He didn't care about his mother's property. With his mother in a coma, there could be no closure. For either of them.

Why on earth am I still here?

Paul's eyes flashed. "She owns a ranch."

Skye's interest perked up. "A ranch?" Thoughts of bronco busting evoked a happy memory from his childhood.

Paul's cell phone rang, and he excused himself to answer it. Skye heard Paul's voice in the corridor as it raised in a heated conversation, but he couldn't make out the words.

When Paul returned, he was still gripping his cell phone.

"This is Ruthanne, Aunt Hannie's assistant. She's been calling every hour to check on her status. She's wondering if you'd like to come out to see the ranch before your meeting tomorrow. It's just south of Oakley. Are you free the rest of the day?"

With his emotions rising up and down like the parachute ride at the county fair, Skye wasn't sure how to answer. On one hand he didn't want to have anything to do with his mother. On the other the thought of visiting a working ranch intrigued him. Dare he step into her world? Who had this woman become after all these years?

With a shrug, he slammed his hands into his pockets. "Sure, why not?"

Paul nodded. "Great. Would you like to see her again before we go?"

The ride plummeted once more. "No."

"Do you mind if I do?"

He hesitated just a moment. "No, of course not." The daily lunch odor wafted from a cart rattling down the corridor and assaulted his nose. Beef broth. His stomach lurched. "I'll meet you in the parking lot and follow you out."

Paul disappeared down the corridor and into the room. Skye rattled his keys all the way to his car.

❧

Ruthanne replaced her phone in her pocket and leaned back against the paddock. She closed her eyes as the humming of the animals and the scent of fresh hay calmed her soul. Lavender from the garden had the same effect.

She needed that sense of serenity right now. Paul hadn't been happy with her suggestion to bring Hannie's son over, but it felt like the right thing to do.

Something woolly brushed her shoulder, and she opened her eyes. She'd just received an alpaca nudge, a reminder that she should be forking the hay instead of inhaling it. You'd think since they grazed all morning that they wouldn't be so testy in the afternoon.

She stroked the alpaca's long russet-colored neck and looked around at the other teddy bear faces surrounding her. They all depended on her now.

As she scooped hay into the first manger, she assured the gathering alpacas that their mommy would be home soon.

Hannie.

Like a mother to her, too. And now Ruthanne could do nothing to save her.

Except pray. She did that a lot lately. Especially since this morning, when she received the call that Hannie would be placed in an induced coma.

She gazed across the green pastureland toward Oregon's Siskiyou Mountains. The verse in Psalms about lifting your eyes to the hills came into her mind, and she drew strength as she recognized the Creator of those hills.

With a prayer on her lips, a strident chorus of outraged alpacas drew her away from her meditation. Harriet, a bossy female who insisted on first dibs at mealtime, had pushed her dapple gray and black body through the group and now lay on the feeding trough so no one else could eat. Ruthanne tried to coax her off but backed away just in time to miss a blast of hay and spit from the alpaca's mouth.

"Okay! Have it your way!" Wheelbarrow in hand, she moved on to the next feeding area. "Sorry, gang, she'll be full soon. Then it'll be your turn."

A roan-colored mother alpaca named Cinnamon chortled from another enclosure, cushing with her legs folded beneath her. She looked like a puffy beanbag pillow with a neck. Her cria romped nearby, playing a game of "let's bounce off Mommy." Baby Payton ran to the farthest side of the pen, turned, and with long, spindly legs loped at full speed toward Cinnamon, landing in her soft fleece and springing off her in a double roll.

Ruthanne welcomed the comedian's antics. She entered

the pen and patted his sandy brown neck. "Laughter is good medicine. I should have named you Isaac."

She forked hay into their trough and moved on to her own alpaca, Lirit. Snowy white—and just as pure of heart. Lirit had a special language all her own. Her humming signaled a contented soul and often soothed Ruthanne's emotions. Hannie had given Lirit to Ruthanne as a cria at an especially tough time in her life, and the two bonded instantly.

Movement on the main road caught her eye. She pulled off her work gloves as she walked between the barn and house and sidestepped the muddy prelandscaped yard to meet them in front. Soon two cars pulled into the circular gravel drive. Paul's blue hybrid whirred in first. The second was a trendy charcoal gray SUV, one the owner would probably never take off-roading. No doubt a gas-guzzler, too.

Ever since Hannie's bombshell, she had puzzled over the mystery surrounding the son. *How did they become estranged? How does he feel about his mother? Does he truly care about her, or will he prove to be a vulture, circling above a victim?*

She shook her head. Not every man was like Brian.

A tall man dressed in business casual—blue khakis and a gray polo shirt—followed Paul up the steps to the porch. By his stormy countenance, he was clearly unhappy. She looked closely to see if he resembled Hannie. Not in the hair. His was dark with a slight wave. The tiny bits of silver told her he was probably in his midforties. Hannie's short crop was blond and straight, although streaked with gray. But as he drew near, she gasped. Those were Hannie's eyes, curious and taking in the surroundings. Looking into his clear blue irises made her wonder if those black clouds circling his head had a silver lining.

Paul greeted her, but his usual cheerful demeanor seemed just as morose as that of their visitor. She felt bad for Paul. With both of his parents gone, Hannie had become a mother to him. His mother's bout with lung cancer no doubt colored his faith now that Hannie suffered from a lung ailment.

She held out her hand. "Hi, I'm Ruthanne Fairfax." She noted the smooth warmth of his hand. He obviously didn't work on a ranch.

A small grin played on his face. "Forgive me, but I thought you would be older."

She flipped her auburn farm-girl braids. Why hadn't she taken more time on her appearance this morning? "The name often fools people. I'm named after my grandmother."

His gaze roved over the house and surrounding land. Ruthanne puffed with pride. "It's something, isn't it?"

"It's beautiful. My. . .mother. . .owns all of this?"

How long ago had this man withdrawn from Hannie's life? "Twenty acres. She and her husband had the house built to their specifications. He worked with the architect, and she made sure her flair was evident."

As they moved inside, Paul asked, "What do you do for a living, Skye?"

"I'm a real estate broker."

Ruthanne spoke over her shoulder. "Then you should be very interested in the construction of this house."

"I noticed the large oak door. That was custom, wasn't it?"

"The whole house is custom built." She nodded toward the sweeping staircase that spilled into the large foyer. "Hand-carved pedestals. There are three bedrooms on the second level, but Hannie's room is on the main level, at the bottom of the stairs." She pointed to the closed door next to the banister.

"That was their original office," Paul interjected. "When Uncle David was diagnosed with multiple sclerosis, they knew he wouldn't be able to navigate the stairs. The office is now a small room off the kitchen. Which is where I'm headed. Ruthanne can show you the rest of the place."

Ruthanne frowned at Paul's retreating figure. There was

nothing pressing in the office.

They moved into the two-story great room, and she nodded toward the massive stone fireplace to the right. "This would be the focal point of the room, but—"

"But"—he finished her thought—"the double french doors are what capture the eye."

Ruthanne was impressed. He seemed to know his stuff. "Yes, the hill behind us is framed in their glass, creating living art. Hannie and David named it Singing Mountain, the same name as our ranch. The locals adopted the name and eventually made it official."

He nodded his approval as he wandered around the room.

Ruthanne pointed upward. "Hannie made sure nothing but natural products were used. Those are real wood beams on the ceiling, not Styrofoam." Then down. "And instead of a plastic product on the floor, she insisted on slate."

"This isn't what I expected."

"What did you expect? Something larger?"

"No. Something more—this sounds strange—psychedelic."

"Ah." Now she understood. "Your mother was a hippie."

"Yes."

She chuckled. "She still is but in a mature, healthy way. Let's see, did she have long blond hair, granny glasses, and flower power?"

If she expected a pleasant reaction from him, she was mistaken. He gave a slight nod, but his nose turned up as if he'd just caught an unpleasant odor; then he turned away and walked toward the french doors. She found herself whiffing the air. Only the cheerful aromas of lilac and forsythia floated in to greet her.

They stepped through the french doors to the redwood back deck where he could view the entire alpaca herd spread out before him. He seized the rail with one hand and pointed with the other. "What are those?"

"Our alpacas."

His face puckered. He watched them grazing, seemingly disappointed with what he saw, yet too fascinated to look away. His slouched posture made her think of a child forced to endure the family vacation.

Under a frown, his eyes searched the grounds. "Aren't there any cows—or horses?"

What was wrong with this guy? Most people found alpacas charming. Perhaps her first instinct had been right, and he was a con artist after Hannie's property. A cattle or horse ranch might be easier to sell.

"No, just alpacas." With a wave, she said, "Oh, we do have some Angora rabbits."

He turned and glared at her. "Rabbits."

Suddenly feeling like a reprimanded child, she pointed weakly to the henhouse attached to the far side of the barn. "And chickens."

He shook his head just a fraction. "Alpacas, rabbits, and chickens."

Was that a snort? How dare he mock something into which Hannie and David had poured heart and soul.

Before she realized it, she placed her hand on her hip and gave him an indignant glare.

"I'm sorry. I expected. . ." His shoulders sagged. "This is all so surreal to me."

Ruthanne suddenly wished she knew more about this man's history. When had he and his mother become estranged? Why hadn't Hannie told her about him? And the question Ruthanne would rather not explore: What about the past had Hannie felt necessary to keep hidden?

two

"Hannie, I met your son." Ruthanne sat by the bedside, saddened that her friend couldn't open her eyes and engage in her animated way. How could such a vibrant woman have been struck down so quickly? It certainly made her think of her own mortality.

She ran her fingers through Hannie's short hair, trying to fluff it the way she always wore it. "Why didn't you tell me about Skye? When he walked into your house yesterday, he acted as if he didn't know you. How long has it been since you've seen him?"

At least three years. That's how long she'd known Hannie, and he'd never visited. Something must have happened. She tried not to judge, but knowing her friend's sweetness and Skye's surliness, he must have been the one to pull away.

"He wasn't there long. I thought he'd want to go into the yard and meet the alpacas up close, but he said he had an appointment." She went on to talk about the alpacas. How they seemed a bit off their feed without her there.

Except Lirit.

How she knew she belonged to Ruthanne was a mystery. Throughout this ordeal, Ruthanne often sat with Lirit long into the evening. Just the thought of her gentle hum calmed Ruthanne's spirit.

She prayed for that same heart song, a physical gauge to know she was in God's will. Tears welled in her eyes. "I know I've thanked you, Hannie, for taking me in and loving me."

And saving my sanity.

Brian had nearly destroyed her. He never made her heart

sing. In those days, seeking God's will was foreign to her.

She flicked a tear off her face and smiled at Hannie. "You sure found a good man though. What was it? Sixteen years of marital bliss before David died? I'll bet you couldn't stop your heart song if you wanted to."

With closed eyes, Ruthanne spoke to God. "Lord, I want a man like David to share my life with. Please send me someone who will make my heart sing." She squeezed Hannie's hand, as if the woman had been praying with her. "Okay now, you have to get well. As my future matron of honor, I can't have you lying around all day."

Paul entered the room, and Ruthanne felt a burn on her cheeks. Had he heard her very private prayer? He avoided looking her in the eye, but he gave no indication when he drew her into the corridor. He offered his usual kiss on her temple and added a gentle squeeze to her shoulder as he led her to the waiting room.

Ruthanne stopped in the middle of the empty room and looked at her friend. His eyes had lost their twinkle. "I'm praying, Paul."

"I know. So am I. But we need to get a grip on reality here."

She shook her head. "Reality is Jesus, and He can heal her."

"Like He healed my mother?"

"It's not the same thing."

Paul rubbed his neck. "I know. Aunt Hannie doesn't have lung cancer."

"I'm sorry about your mother," Ruthanne said. She tried to be sensitive, but Paul grappled with the faith issue in several areas of his life.

He drew her into a hug, but she fisted her arms at her side, stiffening at his touch. Against his shoulder, she asked, "Do you have faith?"

"You know I do, but you also know that faith in God means trusting Him no matter what the circumstances. I've never seen her this sick. What if God chooses to take her home?"

She pulled away to look him in the eyes. "Stop that! She's not a doddering old woman."

Ruthanne grabbed her ears to still the buzzing and sank onto a sofa. The colorless beige cushions reflected the gloom she felt in her heart. She grieved Paul's lack of faith more than Hannie's illness.

Changing the subject, she promised herself to continue to pray for the man until he got it. "Paul. . ." Ruthanne fidgeted with the smooth piping on the couch. "Did you know about Skye?"

He sat next to her and leaned his elbows onto his knees. "No."

"You were young when Hannie married your uncle. You don't remember them talking about him at all?"

He shook his head. "If they mentioned him, I was never aware. After I moved in years later, I'm sure no one mentioned him."

Ruthanne tapped her lip. No mention of an adult child? What had happened to their relationship?

❧

The next day Skye entered the square two-story building to meet Paul and Ruthanne at the lawyer's office. Paul stood just inside the foyer, ending a call on his cell phone.

Skye shook his hand as Paul slipped the phone into his front pocket. "That was Ruthanne. She'll be here in a minute."

They entered through a frosted glass door where a receptionist greeted them. "Please have a seat until your third party arrives. Then you can go in." She pointed to two leather chairs flanking an oak table.

After an awkward silence, Skye started the conversation. "So, you've known my mother how long?" He winced. Even to his own ears, his question sounded like interrogation.

Paul didn't seem fazed. "She married my uncle when I was twelve. I have very few memories of him without her."

Lucky you.

The receptionist spoke into her phone with heated tones. Skye shifted his eyes toward her. "Thank you. I'll expect you this afternoon."

She hung up and addressed Skye, who just realized he'd been staring at her. She pointed toward the ceiling with a pen. "Sorry about the canned music. The speaker's been cutting in and out." She used the pen to air loop her ear. "It's been driving me crazy!"

Music? He hadn't noticed it. Turning back to Paul, he pressed with one more question. "And what about you? Has she been supportive of you all these years?"

Paul's eyebrows shot upward, lines creasing his forehead. "As much as I have been of her." His voice held a defensive edge. "Now *I* have a question."

With a nod, Skye accepted the challenge in his statement.

"Why didn't I know about you?"

Skye ground his teeth. "That's something only my mother can tell you."

Ruthanne entered the room, ending the standoff.

The receptionist stood and led them to a conference room painted in earth tones of green and brown. They each took seats, Paul and Ruthanne on one side and Skye on the other.

A man entered, carrying a folder, and introduced himself to Skye as Vaughn Stanton. The young lawyer looked barely old enough to have passed the bar. Skye shook his hand but must have looked skeptical. "I'm not the Stanton in the partnership. That would be Dad." He pointed to a photo on the wall of three men—Hurst, Hurst, and the elder Stanton. "But someday. . ."

Skye caught Ruthanne's expression in the polished walnut veneer tabletop. Her eyes showed strain. In the brief time he'd known her, Skye had concluded that she was an old soul in a thirty-something's body.

"It's a pleasure to meet you, Mr. Randall," Vaughn Stanton

began as he took his seat at the head of the table. "I've known your mother for several years." He glanced at Paul and raised a questioning eyebrow.

"Go ahead," Paul said. "He might find it interesting to hear how you met Aunt Hannie."

"I don't normally let my clients know this tidbit about my past, but since you're related to the woman who changed my life. . ." He reached out for the folder he had brought into the room. "I was a troubled teen and did community service at your mother's ranch. I fell in love with the animals—and with Hannie. She helped turn me around."

The more the man talked, the more Skye wanted to bolt.

When Skye didn't respond, Vaughn fidgeted with the folder. "Yes, well. . .let's get down to business. When Hannie became ill, I think it frightened her. Perhaps it had to do with losing her husband a few years ago, but for whatever reason, she left clear instructions on what to do if she were incapacitated, even briefly." He brushed each of them with an empathetic gaze. "I'd say a coma qualifies. It is her request, in the event she can't run the ranch, that you, Skye, are made aware of her wishes. Her intention is that you get to know the business."

Skye leaned forward. "Why?"

"Because she wants you to inherit the ranch."

He gripped the arms of the chair. He'd always wanted to own acreage. But could he accept it this way—from this woman? "Assuming I want the ranch, how am I supposed to learn the business? I have a job in Merrick."

"This part isn't going to be easy then. You must stay at the ranch for a minimum of thirty days."

With a force that propelled his chair backward, Skye stood. "Physically?" He stabbed the table with his finger. "On the property?"

The lawyer nodded. "Day and night. It's her wish that you experience the full effect of ownership."

Skye sank back into the chair, the wheels in his brain turning.

"Obviously you'll need a coach." Vaughn nodded toward Ruthanne. "This is where you come in. Hannie has asked that you show Skye around, involve him in the workings of the ranch, and perform business as usual. I'm assuming that Hannie doesn't want any interruption, and she knows you'll need help running it."

Ruthanne nodded. "We have a part-time employee who is out of town at the moment. Paul does what he can, but he has a job. We have events coming up, and I know she doesn't want me to cancel." She chewed her lower lip, no doubt weighing the pros and cons of inviting a stranger to the ranch. Her gaze darted to him, then to her hands clutching each other on the table. She closed her eyes briefly. Was she praying? Finally she drew a breath. "I can definitely use the help."

Skye also sent up a quick prayer. But his analytical mind still had questions. "And what if I refuse? What happens to the ranch then?"

Vaughn closed the file and folded his hands. "In the event of Hannie's death"—Ruthanne squirmed—"which won't be for a long time, but she wants us to think about it now, the ranch will be sold, with 10 percent going to charity and the rest split between Paul and Ruthanne."

Ruthanne turned to look at Paul. Skye suddenly felt like the third wheel. They didn't need him to keep the ranch going—they could hire someone—and if he walked away from the whole thing, they'd come out ahead. Why would Ruthanne even help him learn the business?

Vaughn continued. "And if you accept, please understand that you must continue the workings of the ranch for five years unless it becomes a burden to keep it. If that happens, she asks that you discuss the future of the ranch with Paul and Ruthanne before selling."

This was too weighty a matter for Skye to make a snap decision. "When do you need to know?"

"Take all the time you need, but remember, Ruthanne could use your help now. You could fulfill the one month, and then when"—he glanced at Ruthanne—"or rather, *if* the time comes, you can make the decision to take over for five years."

Skye left, promising to give his answer within the week.

ᔰ

Skye returned to his home in Merrick with a half day to be productive, but he decided instead to take the afternoon off to pray. Changing out of his business attire, he got sloppy with cutoff jeans and a T-shirt.

In the backyard, Ruddy greeted him with a wet kiss. He ruffled the big red dog's ears and looked deep into his brown eyes. "What do you think, boy? They don't know about you. Would everything be called off if I brought my brute?" An Irish setter/Great Dane mix, Ruddy's size alone had caused the neighbors to cross the street, until they got to know him. Ruddy grabbed his Frisbee and frisked about the backyard to entice his master to play. Skye took pity on the dog and tossed the disk around while he talked to God.

At first he laid his feelings out, knowing his Father already understood. "Why would she do this, Lord? Why would she stay out of my life all these years and then offer me her ranch? Her alpaca ranch! Is it a guilt offering?" He decided if that were the case, she must feel horrible for what she'd done to him.

"And what about her nephew and assistant? She embraced them as her family. Why doesn't she just give them the ranch? Why drag me into the middle?"

At one point during his increasingly heated conversation with God, he threw the disk too hard—his attempt at casting his cares, which were heavy—and it landed in the maple tree. The freshly budded leaves grasped it as if capturing their first souvenir of the season. Ruddy whined as he attempted to climb up the trunk, his toy just out of reach.

"Sorry, boy." Skye grabbed a lawn rake and stabbed at the disk until it fell at Ruddy's feet. The grateful dog scooped it up and pranced away, not willing to let his master have the toy again so soon. A game of keep-away ensued, but when Skye tired long before the dog did, he left Ruddy to chew on a rawhide bone while he went inside to chew some more on his own problem.

He sat for a long time, feeling the slight breeze on his face as it drifted in from the open living room window. The normally calming sound of rustling leaves did nothing to relieve his stress. Every argument he could think of bombarded his practical side, and he had just decided to refuse the offer and never think of Hannah again when the phone rang. He looked at the caller ID and answered. "Hi, Mom."

"Hi, honey. How'd it go today? I've been so curious."

Skye laid his Bible aside and silently thanked God for the woman who had chosen him. "Sorry. I came home to pray and think about their offer."

"Offer?"

After relating the crazy thing asked of him, his mom, in an attempt to make things easier, took away his one excuse. "If you need to be there for thirty days, I'm sure it won't be a problem with your dad. You've pulled in more than your quota this year. You deserve a vacation."

Skye gritted his teeth. Why couldn't he work at a regular brokerage house, with a hard taskmaster and a whip? No, he had to go into the family business where TRUST AND OBEY was more than just a phrase on the plaque over the door.

Mom must have sensed his hesitation. "Perhaps you need prayer."

No, I need a ticket out of town.

"Lord, You know how hard this is for my boy. Please give him direction and wisdom, but moreover, Lord, please give him compassion. Only You know what's going on in his heart, and I pray You give him the strength to make this life-changing decision. In Jesus' name. Amen."

Skye's throat tightened through the prayer as conviction squeezed him, but he managed to croak, "Thanks, Mom. You're the best."

"Now while you make this decision. . ."

He smiled. Mom might pray for direction, but no matter how old he became, she'd always keep her hand in shaping his character.

". . .remember that Hannah is a person, too. She deserves prayers as much as anyone else. I hope you've been lifting her before the Lord."

He hadn't.

Mom went on. "Your dad and I have been praying for this woman ever since we adopted you. Now it's time for you to forgive."

He tried to tell Mom what she wanted to hear, but his clenched jaw prevented it. The subject mercifully moved to more mundane things, but the words *"it's time for you to forgive"* continued to ping around in his brain.

When he hung up, he called Vaughn Stanton.

three

On Monday morning Ruthanne stood with Paul on the front porch as Skye pulled into the drive.

Lord, are You sure about this?

Emotions roiled within her as the tires crunched the gravel then stopped. By agreeing to Hannie's wishes, Ruthanne felt as though she were already losing her friend.

She descended the wooden steps, planning to help Skye unload, but before she reached the bottom, a furry red monster came bounding out of the SUV. It rushed at her like a linebacker ready to tackle.

"What is that thing?" She flung the words over her shoulder as she hustled back up the stairs, hoping to hide behind Paul. But her protector had retreated behind the screen door, where she quickly joined him.

"Ruddy! Come here! Bad dog!" Skye called out, taming the wild creature into submission. It slunk back to him with tail tucked under and long ears drooping. "Sit." Skye pointed to the ground where the animal dutifully sat with a huff.

Skye looked up at Ruthanne. "Sorry. You said on the phone that I could bring him."

Ruthanne willed her heart to stop tharumping. "You said he was big, but I didn't realize how big." She cut a sharp glance at Paul.

"What?" Paul motioned with his head toward the animal. "You ran, too."

Skye tapped his hip, and the horse/dog stood. He then paced at his master's side, his long legs like California redwoods.

She watched with a wary eye as the two ascended the stairs.

"What did you call him?"

"Ruddy, for his ruddy complexion. Isn't he a handsome dog?" Skye ruffled the hip-high red head without bending over, causing the ears to whip about in a furry frenzy.

She joined man and dog on the porch, brave now that the beast appeared tame. Ruthanne wasn't short by any means, but this monster's warm breath near her midsection made her feel like a Lilliputian. And he was Gulliver!

Skye stroked the dog's neck. "He's really very gentle. Go ahead and pet him."

She reached out and tapped Ruddy gingerly on the forehead then brought her hand back, dripping with slobber. "My, what a long tongue you have!"

Skye laughed. "The better to kiss you with, my dear." He wiggled a swarthy brow as he handed her his handkerchief, then he pointed to a corner of the porch where he directed Ruddy to sit and stay.

Ruthanne wiped her fingers and handed back the handkerchief. Her stomach fluttered at his teasing. Or was that mild flirting? With her dry hand, she combed her fingers through her braid-free hair, grateful she'd taken time to style it that morning. Maybe she'd be able to endure the coming month after all.

❦

Skye followed Ruthanne into his mother's home.

Lord, are You sure about this?

He imagined himself walking into a large, gaping mouth where his past would consume his present and belch out who knew what of his future.

"Your room is up here." Ruthanne started up the stairs, her patchwork wraparound skirt dusting the steps. On her feet were the ugliest brown shoes he'd ever seen on a woman. She wore a cream-colored knit cardigan to finish the odd ensemble.

Paul followed, carrying the shaving kit and garment bag,

casting dubious looks at Ruddy when he reached the top. Skye brought up the rear, keeping Ruddy in check, knowing his dog would much rather beat everybody to the second floor.

As he placed his foot on the bottom step, he glanced toward his mother's closed bedroom door. He had expected to have some issues living in his mother's house, so his uneasiness near her personal space was no surprise. He hurried up the stairs to join the others.

Ruthanne had disappeared into a room, and Paul, now free of the items he'd carried up, excused himself. "I'll make lunch while you get settled." He skirted around Ruddy on his way back down.

As he entered the room to join Ruthanne, he asked, "Is Paul here all the time? If so, he'd better get used to my dog, or this is going to be one long month for him."

Her fond smile and glance toward the door told him she had feelings for Paul. Just what kind of feelings were they? "Paul lives just a few miles from here, in town."

"So, what's his role, besides being the heir apparent until I came along?"

"When David's MS prevented him from doing the office work, Paul stepped in and took over that role. This put him near the kitchen, so he also became our personal chef to be sure we were all well fed. His real love has always been cooking. It's in his blood. His grandmother owns a restaurant on the coast. He's a chef at the Pine Creek Inn. Have you ever eaten there?"

"No." And if she really wanted to know, he rarely lingered in Oakley because of its strong nonconformist influence. The farther he could get from anything resembling the hippie lifestyle, the better.

He walked over to a large bay window with a blue-cushioned seat. "This is a nice room. Is yours as big as this?"

"This was Paul's room. He moved in with Hannie and David

while he was going to college. His mom had recently died, and David needed help, so it all worked out."

Ruddy proceeded to sniff every object in the room while Skye and Ruthanne stepped through a sliding glass door and onto an upper redwood deck.

"I live in that mobile home on the edge of the property. It was Hannie and David's while they built the house. I've been there for three years, and it's just the right size for me, although Hannie has been trying to get me to move in here." She turned to sit and picked at a thread on the bottom of her shirt. "I'm considering it for when she comes home. She'll probably need help getting around."

She took a big breath and leaned on the deck railing. "Occasionally you will have to come out to investigate things. If you hear the alpacas become agitated, it could be a predator or stray dog in the area."

Skye gazed out on the pleasant ranch scene from the deck, his eyes roving from the barn to the paddocks and out to the pasture where some of the animals munched the grass.

Ruthanne also looked at the panorama but with proud eyes. "Hannie *will* come home to this."

This was the second time Ruthanne had mentioned Skye's mother coming home. He recalled the doctor's assurance that they would try to keep his mother in the surviving percentile. But then he also remembered Paul's defeated slump. Her odds weren't that great with just over half a chance to survive. "How can you be so sure that's going to happen?"

Ruthanne grimaced and seized the rail. "I have faith."

Was she a believer? He had to know. "In Jesus?"

Her eyes misted. "Absolutely. And in Hannie."

She turned to him. "What about you?"

"I have faith in Jesus." He'd lost faith in his mother.

He walked back into his room to give Ruthanne a private moment. "Ruddy! Off!" Grateful he'd given his dog a bath just yesterday, Skye nevertheless brushed the window seat cushion where Ruddy had claimed his spot. The dog obeyed, but Skye knew this would be an ongoing battle. He whipped out his handkerchief and rubbed the nose prints off the window.

Ruthanne came through the door, hugging her body with one arm and wiping at her cheeks with the other.

He changed the subject. "Do alpaca ranches pay that well?" He couldn't imagine how alpaca breeding could garnish enough income for such a palace.

"It does very well, but David had the means to be able to afford most of this before he married Hannie."

My mother's a gold digger, too?

Ruthanne walked out of the room. "If you need anything else, please let me know. I'll leave you to unpack, then we can have lunch."

She disappeared before he could say thank you. Was she still emotional over his mother, or did she feel as awkward about the situation as he did?

☙

As Ruthanne left Skye, she wanted to think the best of him. Had he asked about the income because he was considering keeping the ranch? Or was he calculating its worth for when he sold it? *Please, Lord, no.* She wanted to like Skye for Hannie's sake.

During lunch she had to struggle to keep from laughing at Paul. With Ruddy sprawled in one corner of the kitchen, Paul sat where he could watch him, keeping his back to the wall.

When they were through, Paul showed Skye the room off the kitchen. Ruthanne could hear him while she cleared the table. "This is our business office. I've been cataloging Aunt Hannie's weavings for Internet sales."

Ruthanne filled the dishwasher while thinking of the Internet portion of the business. Paul had been such an asset since his uncle's death, and the online sales were his idea. She was grateful he took an active part, because she had enough to do just to keep the ranch running.

Perhaps it was good that Hannie had requested Skye be contacted.

He came back into the kitchen, pointing his thumb over his shoulder. "Are there enough books on alpacas in there? Or do you need to stock up on some more?"

She smiled. "When you realize Hannie and David started from scratch, not knowing a thing about alpacas, it's no wonder they own every book on the subject. Did you see the bookshelf that contained craft books?"

"You could start a library. Does my mother make all the crafts?"

"Most. She's the artist. Her weavings tell a story. You can see them throughout the house, but most are downstairs in the shop. I've made some things, too, but they're not the same quality." She dried her hands on a towel. "You ready to try your dog outside?"

"Are you sure?" Skye glanced at Ruddy.

No, she wasn't sure. "We have to test him around the alpacas sooner or later. He was so well behaved during lunch—let's try him on the deck at first. Do this slowly. Maybe tomorrow I can put the alpacas in the barn and introduce him to each one separately."

"Okay." Skye tapped his hip. "Let's go, Ruddy."

The dog rose from his prone position in the corner of the kitchen and took his place beside Skye.

With a mischievous tone, she called out to Paul, who had holed himself up in the office. "Would you like to come with us?"

His muffled voice drifted to them. "Depends. Where is the black demon?"

"In the far pasture."

After a pause, he called out again. "That's okay. I have stuff to do here."

She chuckled as she led Skye down the stairs off the deck. "He's referring to Gabriel." She pointed to the magnificent alpaca standing alone at the far fence. Long, pitch-black dreadlocks flowed from his back, and he held his head high, as if he knew they were admiring him. Framed by the rising mountain behind him, the view would have made a perfect postcard. "For reasons known only to God, Gabriel has waged war on Paul. He grunts and spits whenever he comes near."

They stopped on the back deck and allowed Ruddy a view of the alpacas. Skye remained alert as his dog spotted them. His tail and legs went stiff, and he began to *wuff* softly.

"Easy, boy. It's okay—they belong here." Skye patted the dog's head.

Ruddy sat but continued to whine. Ruthanne breathed a sigh of relief—but too soon. Apparently it was too much for the dog. He let out an earsplitting howl as he bounded down the steps toward the pasture.

"Ruddy! Heel! Heel! Come here!" Skye sprinted after the dog but couldn't catch up to him.

Ruthanne brought up the rear, hiking her skirt to her knees, intent on protecting her animals. In horror she watched Ruddy sail over the fence. Gabriel advanced.

"Skye, get him away from Gabriel!"

Ruddy ran and barked as if trying to rally a group to play softball, but Gabriel clearly didn't want to play. He charged, stopped short of running the canine over, and spit.

Ruthanne winced. Green slime on a red dog was not at all festive. Ruddy got the message. He pivoted, jumped back over the fence with the finesse of a hurdler, and headed for the deck. A giggle rose in her throat. Ruddy stood trembling on the deck, and Skye loped up the steps two at a time, scolding the dog all the way.

Paul came out onto the deck, laughing so hard tears had come to his eyes. "See? I told you he was a black demon!"

Skye felt the heat rise out of his collar. Ruddy had never done this sort of thing before. But then again, he'd never seen anything as strange as an alpaca.

"I'm so sorry. I don't know what got into him."

Ruthanne joined him on the deck and dabbed at her perspiring lip with the back of her hand. "No harm done," she wheezed. "I doubt he'll mess with the males anymore. I think we've all learned a lesson."

Together they managed to get Ruddy back down the steps. Skye hosed the vile-smelling slime off his dog, despite Ruddy's quivering throughout the process and casting side-glances toward Gabriel. When Skye turned off the water, Ruddy shook off the excess and loped back to the deck.

"I'll tie him up there."

Ruthanne placed her hand on his arm before he could leave to get Ruddy's leash. "Wait. Look at him."

Ruddy sat in the farthest corner he could find away from the alpacas. A wet sewer rat wouldn't have looked more pitiful.

"I don't think he's going anywhere." Ruthanne giggled.

Skye slid his hands into his back pockets. "I think you're right. What a chicken."

"Go easy on him. He's just had a traumatic experience. Maybe it was a good thing. Look who's just made a new friend." Paul knelt next to the dog, offering him what looked like a leftover piece of veal cutlet from lunch. "I think they've found common ground."

If this continued, he knew he'd have a spoiled dog on his hands. But the pampering was all worthwhile if he didn't have to tether him every time Paul was around.

They walked to the paddocks. He was surprised that they didn't smell that bad. Kind of like hay. Even the droppings seemed to be all neat and tidy in one community pile.

Ruthanne must have noticed him looking at them. "Alpacas

are fairly clean animals. They all go in one place, which is great for you."

"I'll be shoveling that," he stated.

"Yep."

She led him through the paddocks attached to two sides of the barn. The paddocks each had access into the barn and were really one large pen with movable fences. "We keep things portable so we can either segregate or bring everybody together. It's also easier going from one paddock to the other when we don't have to go into the barn to get to each stall."

He liked the system and could see how it would make life easier than walking from the paddock clear around to one central door.

Ruthanne entered a pen where four babies romped near their mothers. "Little ones are called crias, and the moms are dams." A mother and baby were fenced away from the rest. "This is our newborn that came into the world yesterday. We've named her Princess."

The fawn-colored infant looked like a lamb with short, curly fleece and an extremely long neck. She stood with steady, capable legs but never strayed from her mother.

"She sure seems strong." A grin tugged at Skye's lips.

"They get their strength fast. We were keeping her from the other babies until we were sure she could hold her own. She seems to be doing fine, so why don't we try putting them together?"

She untied the fences, and the other mothers and young ones swarmed the newborn. Mom alpaca did her best to keep everyone at a respectable distance by getting between her baby and the well-wishers.

"See these three male crias rushing up to see what the fuss is all about?"

Skye could imagine the three boys as human, tumbling all over each other and trying to engage the smaller children in a game of roughhouse. The new baby hid behind her mother.

Ruthanne continued her tour. "Alpacas are easy and fun animals to work with. Occasionally one needs special attention, so we play vet when we have to."

One curious mother grunted as she eyed Skye with black, nearly pool-ball-sized eyes. She came up to him, apparently just to get a better view, because she shied away when he reached out to touch her.

"Alpacas don't like to be touched on their heads, but it's okay to stroke their necks or backs." Ruthanne handed him a peanut. "Give this to her, and she'll be your best friend."

He did so and was surprised at the stiff hair on her chin. It looked soft but had a slight prick to it. Pliant lips scooped the peanut into the alpaca's mouth.

They moved through the pen with the mama following now, hoping for another peanut.

Ruthanne continued on, introducing each animal as if it were part of the family. "We breed both suris and huacayas here."

"Wa-*who*-ahs?"

"Huacayas." She regarded him as if he were a toddler learning how to talk. "Repeat after me. Hwa. . .ki. . .ah."

As she pronounced the word, he found watching her naturally rosy lips enjoyable. He continued saying the word wrong until she gave up.

"You'll get it eventually," she huffed.

She pointed to a chocolate brown animal. "This is Hershey. You can tell she's a suri by the dreadlocks. Her sire is Gabriel."

"I can see that these animals are in the camel family by the way they sit."

"Yes, llamas and alpacas are in the camelid family. When they sit on their legs like that, it's called cushing."

Hershey rose from her folded position and joined them. Skye reached out to touch the strands of dense wool flowing from the animal's body. After the coarse chin hair, he found it much softer than it looked. "Is her mother brown?"

"No, believe it or not, her mother is white. No one knows why they throw their color the way they do. We were only mildly surprised when black and white equaled brown. In fact, alpacas are bred in twenty-two official colors."

"Impressive."

"The huacayas look like teddy bears." She came to a white animal that rose from the ground to greet her. They nuzzled each other's faces. "This is Lirit. She's mine...or I'm hers." She shrugged. "We belong to each other."

He reached out to touch Lirit's fuzzy fleece but stopped short. The intelligence in her huge black eyes unnerved him. With a small snort, she shied away from his touch and trotted to the far corner of the pen.

Ruthanne frowned. "That's odd. She's usually friendly with strangers. Well, alpacas often remind me of cats in their behaviors"—she waggled a finger in Lirit's direction— "*and* in their independent natures."

They moved on. "This is the boys' hangout. These five are fully grown but still teenagers." Two of the males seemed engaged in a power game, pushing at each other, the long necks dueling like flexible, fuzzy swords.

"What are they fighting about?" Skye winced as the brown one nipped at the cream-colored alpaca's left flank.

Ruthanne didn't seem concerned. "They love to roughhouse, seeing who has hair on his chest. The dark one is Winston, and the light one is Chester. They were born only six weeks apart and got along when they were younger, but now they're establishing the pecking order. Chester is bigger, so I imagine he'll win. We trim their teeth regularly so no one draws blood."

This little tussle actually pleased Skye. He was afraid these animals were as frail as they looked.

Ruthanne spread her arms wide. "This is it—Singing Mountain Ranch."

"I have to admit, it's impressive." Skye found himself looking forward to working on the ranch, even if there weren't cows or horses.

On their way back to the house, Skye asked, "How did you start working with alpacas?"

Ruthanne took a deep breath. "I'm so blessed to be working here. I met Hannie at a craft fair. My husband and I had recently moved here from California."

Husband?

He noticed her enthusiasm over the animals didn't translate when talking about her husband. The spark left her eyes.

She continued. "We'd been living in a small apartment in Oakley—barely making it. Brian was an artist but didn't make much money. Hannie and I clicked. Our booths were located next to each other, and the alpaca there took to me right away. After I confided in her, she consulted David, whose MS had magnified, and he agreed to let us stay in the mobile home on their property if Brian and I would help out." She pointed to the far end of the pasture.

"I haven't met your husband. Is he traveling on the fair circuit?"

The spark returned, but it flashed hot. "No. He's. . . I'm a widow."

"I'm sorry."

She turned her moss green eyes to him, eyes almost as big as those of the alpacas she loved. "Don't be."

Without further explanation she moved on with her shoulders squared, apparently ready for a fight. Subject closed.

They walked into the herdsire paddock. "These guys are our prize sires, dads to most of the animals here."

He glanced out toward the pasture at the majestic black that bested his dog. "Why isn't Gabriel with the other sires?"

"He's an import from South America. Down there, they don't allow the interaction like we do here. He never developed social skills and likely won't. We've just gotten him to the point where he'll let us near, except Paul, of course. Where he's from, humans treat them like animals."

Skye laughed. "I hate to tell you this. . ."

"I know." She giggled, and he found the sound as relaxing as the wind chimes on the deck. "They are all my family."

"Especially. . .what did you call her?"

"Lirit. Hannie gave her to me after my husband left."

Left?

Did they have more than his mother in common? Had Ruthanne been abandoned, too?

four

Not even a week from the time he first learned about his mother, Skye awoke in her house to the discordant *buzz* of his travel alarm. Through blurry vision from a short night's sleep, he saw the numbers: 7:00. He groaned.

Ruddy's snore rumbled from his doggy cushion at the foot of the bed. Skye reached for his Zane Grey paperback book on the nightstand and tossed it at the animal, hitting his right flank. Ruddy merely lifted his head, snorted, and lay back down again.

"Oh no you don't. We're in this together." He stood and slapped his thigh.

Ruddy dragged himself to all fours slowly, acting more like an old man than the teenager he was.

The pair went downstairs to the kitchen, where Skye found a covered plate and a note on the counter. The note read "Skye, Paul made these orange and cranberry bagels. Cream cheese in the fridge. Help yourself and then come on out to the barn. —R"

Ruthanne had told him yesterday that she normally started her day with a light breakfast while she read her Bible. Then by eight o'clock, she would start her chores. He thought that sounded like a good idea.

He released Ruddy outside, and the dog cast a wary eye toward the far pasture where he'd had his altercation with Gabriel. It wasn't long before he loped back up to the house. Skye knew Ruddy wouldn't stray as long as he was near. However, in lieu of keeping the dog sequestered in the bedroom where he could do some damage, Skye would have to figure out a way to keep him in the yard if he'd be gone for any length of time.

After breakfast and a distracted devotion—it was hard to focus on God while sitting in his mother's kitchen—he changed out of the sweatpants and T-shirt he wore to sleep in. Leaving Ruddy on the deck, huddled into his safety spot by the door, he rubbed the soft, red head. "Sissy."

He sought out Ruthanne, who met him in the first stall. Two braids lay stiffly on either side of her head, and she wore a blue oversized man's flannel shirt that drooped to the knees of her faded jeans. These she had stuffed into unattractive green rubber boots. He had to admit she actually looked cute, like a little girl wearing her daddy's clothes.

After greeting him, she handed him a gallon-sized plastic milk container with the spout cut off for scooping and showed him where the grain was located. "We feed them vitamin-fortified grain in the morning then hay about midday and in the evening."

As they entered each stall, alpacas swarmed them like curious hummingbirds.

Fuzzy faces inspected Skye for food, but finding none, they concentrated their attention on Ruthanne.

"I'm very popular this time of day." She grinned.

"I can see that." Skye soon had his turn in the next stall. It seemed they didn't care who brought the food. Their favorite person was whoever made up the waitstaff for that day.

When they finished, she pointed at his feet. "I hope those aren't good shoes."

"No, they're new, but I bought them for here." He wiggled his toes in the leather work boots, already feeling like a ranch owner. "I thought of buying cowboy boots, but since there are no cows or horses, I thought these would be more appropriate."

She accepted his good-natured teasing by handing him a rake and a shovel, effectively deflating his romantic dreams of owning a real ranch. "Here, we'll start with this. Grab that wheelbarrow over there, and I'll show you how to harvest beans."

"Beans?"

She leaned close. "Alpaca poop."

He tossed the garden tools into the wheelbarrow with a clatter and grabbed the rough wooden handles. He then followed her to the corner of the stall where the pellet-sized "beans" lay in a tidy nest of hay. "Seriously? You call them beans?"

He loved her laughter. It was genuine and came so easily. "Believe it or not, that's the acceptable term in our circle."

Skye rolled his eyes, hoping to elicit another giggle from her. She didn't disappoint him.

Once his wheelbarrow was full of beans, she showed him the compost pile where he could dump all of it.

"Nothing's wasted, huh?"

"Nothing." She said it with conviction. Apparently she'd become as much of a tree hugger as his mother had. "We clean the stalls and paddocks in the morning and then again in the evening. This makes it more pleasant not only for us but also for the animals. Alpacas like to be clean."

They finished, and Ruthanne looked at her watch.

"Think you can gather eggs while I start breakfast?"

Even though he'd never been alone with a live chicken, he didn't think it would be hard. However, after she left, he found an overprotective hen who squawked and flapped until he feared she'd hurt herself. He needn't have feared her frailty, though. Her hard beak left peck marks on his hands as he removed her eggs, leaving him to wonder why she thought she had laid them there in the first place.

He took the eggs back to the house in a feminine wicker basket with a red gingham bow attached to the handle, muttering under his breath. "A real man brands cattle and breaks horses. Beans. Eggs. Fluffy bunnies. Bah!"

When he entered the kitchen, Ruthanne stood at the counter slicing oranges. She'd shed the man's shirt, revealing a clean, pink T-shirt. He thought she'd suspended the Bohemian look to work outside, but when she turned, he saw the left waist of the shirt had been tie-dyed yellow and green. Blue socks, a solid color, covered her feet.

She padded over to him and took the basket. "Take your boots off outside, please."

"Oh! Sorry."

"That's okay. There's a bench near the door, and you can just shove your shoes under it."

When he returned, she grinned at him. "I hope you like omelets." She stood, whipping the eggs in a bowl with a fork, the shells tossed into a small bucket on the counter. No doubt a compost pile somewhere awaited the scraps. "I'm always famished by midmorning."

His stomach growled. "If I get omelets every day, I won't mind the chicken abuse."

She snickered. "Guess I'll have to show you how to extract eggs without ruffling feathers."

Skye rubbed his sore hands. "That would be nice."

After breakfast Ruthanne pulled on the ugly boots but left the man's shirt behind, entreating him to follow her. "I'd like you to help me exercise the animals."

He looked out at the acre-wide pasture as they passed the barn. "Don't they get enough exercise running around out there?"

On the far side of the barn, they walked to a round, fenced-in area with short wooden obstacles laid out strategically.

"This course is mostly for our show animals. It helps them get used to maneuvering through doors or other things they'll encounter away from the ranch. This is also an opportunity to teach them to be haltered and work with a lead." She pointed to what looked like flat debris near the far fence.

"That bit of roofing is where we walk all our alpacas who are skittish about the scales they get weighed on. With the various objects we have here and the roofing, it teaches them not to be frightened when they encounter something strange under their feet."

Wouldn't horses be easier?

They entered a paddock where a gray-fringed alpaca eyed them warily. Ruthanne approached him despite his grunts to warn her away. "This is Silver Bullet."

"I like the name. The Lone Ranger only used bullets made of valued silver to show his desire to value life and only shoot to maim."

"You know some strange trivia, Skye Randall." She shook her head.

"Don't get me started on Roy Rogers."

"Don't worry." She held up her hand. "I won't."

During the course of the next hour, Skye learned how to put a halter on Silver Bullet and how to exercise him by walking him over and through the obstacles.

Ruthanne sat on the fence while Skye put Silver through his paces. "Are you feeling comfortable with him yet?"

"Who are you talking to, Silver or me?" Even though the alpaca was smaller than a horse, Skye felt the power in his long neck.

"Both, I guess." Her intriguing laughter floated on the still air. "One last obstacle and you can bring Silver over here. I need to tell you about what's happening on Friday."

Silver stepped over a block without fighting for control and allowed Skye to lead him to Ruthanne. She hopped off the fence and patted Silver's neck, praising him for a job well done.

"Hey, what about me?" Skye feigned hurt feelings.

Ruthanne reached up to touch his neck but pulled her hand back. "You, too." Her cheeks glowed an attractive pink.

What would her hand feel like? Calloused and rough or as

gentle as her alpacas?

"Anyway." She cleared her throat and opened the gate to release Silver into the pasture. "The ranch is hosting a field trip for the area schoolchildren. They arrive throughout the day in buses. We give them a tour then hold a little craft time with them in the large room off the gift shop."

Skye clenched the gate, the cool metal quickly warming from his sweaty palm. "Wait a minute. All day you've been saying 'we' when it's actually been me doing all the work."

"That won't be the case on Friday." She laughed. "Usually I do the tour and Hannie does the craft segment while showing them how she weaves on her loom. They make their own little weavings that turn out like lopsided coasters. But it teaches them how to work with alpaca fiber."

Did she honestly think he could teach them how to weave? "I'm not qualified for either job."

Ruthanne waved her hand. "Don't worry. I'll do both, and the teachers know how to do the craft, so they can supervise that. Paul will feed the kids, something he looks forward to every year. I'll just need you to move things along and make the animals behave. After this week is over, you'll be fairly comfortable with them."

Throughout the week her words proved correct. Skye found he could halter even the most obstinate creature and lead it through its paces without difficulty.

As the buses approached on Friday morning, he prayed he would be as comfortable around the children.

"Sorry, boy," he said to Ruddy, who strained against the chain attached to a spike in the yard. "This was the best I could come up with. I don't want you scaring the kids. Maybe I'll let you play with them after they get used to you."

Ruddy's sharp whine nearly made Skye change his mind. But then he turned the corner of the house. Excited children spilled out of the vehicles, scurrying like ants from a crushed hill. His dog would only add chaos to chaos, he feared. Teachers and parent volunteers managed to corral them, and somehow Skye and Ruthanne filtered them out to the pasture for their tour.

Ruthanne had chosen the more docile alpacas to interact with the group. Even so, their guttural grunts sounded a warning as the intruders gathered on the far side of the fence. Soon most of the alpacas greeted the children, their necks stretched toward them in curiosity, as if they'd never seen a human that short before. Once the two sides were comfortable with each other, Ruthanne opened a gate and allowed the group in for their up close and personal tour.

Skye marveled at Ruthanne's stamina as she led several groups through the premises at intervals. *Her ugly earthy shoes must support her feet pretty well.* She'd opted for jeans with a beautiful woven belt. Turquoise beads threaded on strings hung off the belt and hit her hips when she walked. Her gauzy tunic top made her look as young as some of the sixth graders.

Even though the tour was the same Ruthanne had given Skye, he learned so much more because the children thought to ask questions he'd never dreamed of.

"Why don't they have pupils in their eyeballs?"

"They have them," Ruthanne answered. "But because their eyes are so dark, you can't see them."

"Why do some of them look like my shaggy dog and others look like my Chia Pet?"

Ruthanne pulled one of the alpacas near. "This shaggy dog is a suri. Her hair has no crimp and grows down from her body in pencil-like dreadlocks." She dug into the coat and let the children see what she was talking about. Then she wrapped her arms around the neck of another alpaca. "This Chia Pet is a huacaya. Her fiber does have crimp so it springs from her body. It's fuzzier and very soft." Again everybody felt deep into the coat and watched how the layers bounced out.

One little boy recoiled. "Ew. It's just like my sister's hair!"

"Speaking of hair. . ." Ruthanne reached to her own head and pulled a strand out. "I want everyone to grab a hair. . . from your own heads, please."

Giggles and then yelps of pain followed.

"Now compare it to the alpaca hair."

Skye, feeling like one of the kids, dug into the wool and compared his hair with the alpacas. The silkiness of the alpaca hair reminded him of a cat.

"Hair is measured in microns. The thinner the hair, the lower the micron."

One boy raised his hand. "What's a micron?"

"It's a type of measurement, like inches or yards. But a micron is very tiny."

His teacher addressed the group. "We'll go back to class and learn about microns so you can understand what Miss Ruthanne is talking about." She smiled at Ruthanne, who looked relieved at not having to go into great detail.

"The human hair measures around sixty to one hundred microns," Ruthanne continued. "Alpaca hair measures sixteen to thirty microns. Plus, its hollow core makes it smooth and light."

She let this sink in before continuing. "Your grandpa's socks made from sheep's wool are much heavier and itchier than alpaca socks."

At one point during Ruthanne's talk about why alpacas hum, one nine-year-old girl held up her hand. "I like to hum when I'm happy. Do they hum when they're happy?"

"Some do, some don't," Ruthanne answered. "They have a unique language that includes grunts for distress or gentle humming as they talk to each other. Even though they love kids, you probably heard them when you walked up. Can you make that same sound?"

They all tried, most sounding like little pigs.

Ruthanne continued. "There is one special alpaca that loves everybody and seems to hum when she's happy." She sifted through the alpacas. "This is Lirit. Her name means 'lyrical' in Hebrew. The owner of the ranch, Hannie Godfrey, takes Lirit to nursing homes, orphanages, and prisons. Lirit helps people learn to love again. Hannie gave her to me at a very special time when I needed a good friend. Have you ever talked to a pet about your problems?"

While the children chattered about their own pets, a mother chaperone pulled Ruthanne aside. Skye, who stood nearby, made a point to listen when he heard his mother's name mentioned. "Hannie visited my father at Northwoods Senior Center a few months ago." The woman suddenly had tears in her eyes. "She brought Lirit. He always had a soft spot for animals. For the first time in his life, Dad allowed someone—Hannie—to tell him about God. He accepted Christ as his Savior that day. The next week he passed away."

Both women were in tears now, but they quickly swiped them away before the children saw them.

This was the first Skye had heard that his mother had become a Christian. But had she really? She'd used that line before to get some quick cash from an innocent pastor, with five-year-old Skye by her side to make her look respectable.

What game was she playing this time?

Ruthanne's lilting voice brought him back to the present. "Listen. Lirit loves all of you. Hear her hum?"

Skye was standing back a ways, apparently too far to hear Lirit. Then again, he never remembered hearing the alpaca hum. He'd been working on the ranch for a week, and all he got from sweet Lirit was attitude.

The children moved on to the classroom where crafts and Paul's snacks awaited them. Skye lingered near the alpaca. "So, what is it about me that you don't like, girl?" He offered her a peanut, one of many he kept in his pocket. She regarded him as if he'd lost his mind, turned her back, flattened her ears, and effectively ignored him.

"I don't get it," he muttered as he joined the rest of the group.

୧

As the last bus pulled away, Ruthanne stood in the driveway and waved. She couldn't wait to sit on the back deck and put her feet up. She loved children, but she'd never hosted so many classes by herself before.

She had just eased herself down on a deck chair when Skye showed up with a tray of punch-filled glasses and a plate of small sandwiches.

"Thanks. These aren't the whipped peanut butter and jelly bean ones that Paul made for the kids, are they?" She carefully lifted the top half of the croissant, fully expecting to see a purple piece of candy nestled inside. "He gets imaginative around holidays, and jelly beans are his favorite Easter candy."

"No, these are chicken salad. He said you'd like it." Skye plopped into the chair next to her.

Ruthanne took a healthy bite, savoring the mixture of walnuts and sweet dried cranberries. She hadn't realized how hungry she'd become.

Once her unfed stomach stopped grousing, she noticed Skye's haggard face. "You look as tired as I feel. Thank you for filling in the gap. I never realized how hard this would be without Hannie."

He tilted his mouth as if he were going to say something but must have changed his mind.

Trying to fill the ensuing silence, Ruthanne found herself babbling. "I love children. They're so curious, and the whole world is before them, waiting to be discovered. What about you? Do you like kids?"

"Sure. If I ever have one of my own, I'll protect him and always make him feel special."

Nothing particularly odd about that statement, but the haunted look in his eyes disturbed Ruthanne. It passed quickly, though, so she continued the train of thought. "Have you ever been married, Skye?"

"Nope, never found one who would put up with me."

She found that hard to believe. After watching his work ethic and his gentlemanly ways, she suspected he had some mighty high standards of his own. "If I get married again, I'd love to have a boy and a girl. One of each."

Paul stepped through the door from the kitchen and plopped onto a deck chair. After preparing the snacks, serving them, and playing with the kids, he'd worked as hard as they had. He continued their conversation. "Two kids sounds great. A child for each lap. No one fighting over who gets to sit by the window in the car."

Skye smiled for the first time since they'd begun talking about children. "You two have obviously never grown up in a big family."

"And you have?" Ruthanne leaned forward. Maybe she'd finally get some of her questions answered.

"I'm the oldest of five kids."

"But. . ." Ruthanne glanced at Paul who simply blinked back at her. "Hannie never mentioned having children. Then again, she never talked much about her life before marrying David."

"No, she wouldn't have done that, would she?" Skye thrust himself from his chair and stood at the deck railing with his back to them. His shoulders tensed like two cement blocks on either side of his spine. When he turned around, he seemed to be willing himself to relax. "I was adopted. My family consists of two awesome Christian parents and four sisters. The others are my parents' natural offspring, but they always treated me like blood."

She moved to stand next to him and leaned on the railing.

Reaching out to touch his arm, she tentatively asked, "How old were you when you were adopted?"

"Thirteen."

That answered why she hadn't seen him around. And from Hannie's testimony, she guessed someone had removed him from the home due to drug abuse. However, that didn't answer why Hannie never told her, or even Paul, about him. Only Hannie could satisfy that question.

five

"It's been a week. How do you feel about the ranch?" Ruthanne asked Skye during breakfast on Monday.

With everything he needed to do, his days flew by. It surprised him that he only had three weeks left. "It's not as hard as I thought it would be. I'll admit, I'm having fun."

"Even without bronco busting and cattle branding?"

"Okay, I thought alpaca ranching would be lame. . . ."

"And?" Her eyes twinkled, making him glad he'd shared his disappointment with her.

"And that no real man should be caught dead shoveling their, er, beans."

"Wait until one of them gives birth. If you can survive that, you will be a real alpaca rancher."

He shuddered at the thought. "I remember you showing me the pregnant ones. How many did you say are due in the next three weeks?"

"Only four of them."

Skye groaned. *Any way they could all be overdue, Lord?*

"Relax, a couple of them have a habit of waiting a month then surprising us when we least expect it. And they do most of the work." Ruthanne rose and took her plate to the sink. "Would you like to see your mother today? I thought I'd go this afternoon."

Nearly every day she asked if he'd go with her to the hospital, and he always came up with excuses.

"Actually I need to drive into Merrick today. Check out my house, make sure the plants haven't died."

She turned with the dish towel wrapped around her hands.

"Would you mind if I tagged along? I can see Hannie this evening. I need to get some supplies for the craft fair next weekend. Mundane stuff, like PVC pipe and plastic crates."

"Sure, if you don't mind being gone the whole day. My parents have invited me out to lunch."

"Oh." She waved the towel then turned to wipe the counter dry. "I don't want to intrude."

Intrusive was the last thing Ruthanne could be. Her gentle spirit had often calmed his soul this past week as his emotions churned like a thunderstorm. He smiled. "I would love to have you come and meet my folks."

Ruthanne replaced the towel on its wooden rack by the sink, leaned on the counter, and drew lazy circles on the granite finish. "I don't know. . . ."

Seeing her hesitation, he decided to seal the deal. "You'd be doing me a favor. I'm bombarded with questions whenever I talk to my mom on the phone. She's curious about the alpacas, and it would be great if she could talk to the expert."

The finger circling stopped, and she gently tapped the counter. "Okay. If you're sure they won't mind."

Skye whipped out his cell phone. After briefly apprising his mom of the change in plans, he hung up and smiled. "She can hardly wait."

❧

After her chores Ruthanne cleaned up to prepare for her day with Skye. He wanted to leave at 11:00, but at 10:55 she was still standing in front of her closet without a clue of what to wear.

She was going to put on jeans and her favorite peasant blouse to visit Hannie, but now that seemed frumpy. Finally she grabbed a robin's egg blue top and a midcalf-length broom skirt with a peacock-feather pattern. The spring day had started to warm nicely, so she opted for her green ballet-type slippers.

As she assessed herself in the mirror, she felt silly. Why should she worry about what to wear the first time she met Skye's mom? Even so, she brushed out her braids and fluffed her hair so it fell past her shoulders, adding vintage chandelier earrings. Before walking out of her bathroom, her hand hesitated over her sparse makeup bag. She opened it slowly, feeling as though someone else was guiding her hand. Repeating to herself *Silly, silly, silly,* she dusted her face with translucent powder to dull the freckles and swiped on the pearl pink lipstick she'd bought last year for an event honoring Hannie. With a last check in the mirror, she left her trailer and walked the gravel path between the pastures.

When she entered the back door, she called for Skye. He was on the front porch, waiting for her.

"I'm sorry." She fingered her skirt, suddenly self-conscious. "I felt I needed to change if we were going out to lunch."

Skye took in her appearance, coolly appraising her. No compliment for her efforts?

"No problem. You're right on time." She followed him to his car, wondering about his mood swing.

❧

Skye glanced at the woman sitting next to him. Why did she have to wear *that*? He'd become used to Ruthanne's hippie clothing while at her house, but she was about to visit *his* world. The last thing he wanted to do was infest it with anything that resembled his birth mother.

When they arrived at the restaurant, Skye opened his car door, but Ruthanne flipped the visor and checked her makeup in the vanity mirror—something Skye had never seen her do before. In fact, he'd never seen her in makeup. She looked fine without it.

As Skye accompanied Ruthanne inside, buttery garlic smells swirled around them. "This is my favorite Italian restaurant." His stomach growled, punctuating his comment. The hostess led them to the table where his parents waited, and they both rose to hug him.

"Mom, Dad, this is Ruthanne Fairfax."

His dad held out his hand and pumped Ruthanne's arm. Mom drew her into a hug. Over Ruthanne's shoulder she mouthed the words, "She's cute," to which Skye mouthed back, "Don't even think about it."

Feminine, young adult arms wrapped around his waist.

Without looking back, he said, "And this would be my baby sister, Robyn."

"Hey, big bro!"

She unwound her arms and curtsied. "You're Ruthanne. Pleased to meet you. I'll be your waitress this afternoon."

As they scooted into the booth, she took their drink orders then disappeared less enthusiastically than she had appeared.

"Our little actress," Mom explained. "Waitressing pays her bills, but she's getting a performing arts degree at the university."

"The campus in Oakley?" Ruthanne picked up her napkin and removed the utensils before placing it in her lap. "Has she been to the Shakespeare Festival?"

"Frequently." Dad rolled his eyes.

Mom playfully slapped his shoulder. "Acting runs in my family. My brother is a producer in Hollywood." She waved her hands. "But I want to know about the ranch."

Most people bombarded Mom when she confessed about the thespian half of her family, but today, as Skye had predicted, Mom had plenty of her own questions.

"I'm fascinated with the process of taking the wool and turning it into those colorful yarns I see in the craft stores."

"And boy, it is a process, too." Ruthanne laughed. "A long one. Hannie used to do all of the carding and dying herself, but now she sends the fiber out to be done. There are people who specialize in just that. Then we get it back, and she spins it into those yarns you see. This weekend we're participating in a craft fair in Oakley. Please come out if you can. I'll be doing demonstrations all day of how we go from the animal to the finished product."

"Oh, I'd love that. I hope you're selling some things made from your own alpacas."

"Absolutely. That's part of the fun."

Skye and his dad glanced at each other and smiled. Mom loved crafty things but only had the patience to learn scrapbooking.

By the time the main course arrived, Ruthanne had invited his parents to the ranch for a tour. They settled on a date, contingent on Hannie's health.

"Skye." His mother finally acknowledged his presence. "We have a favor to ask."

"I knew it." He smacked the table. "You've been plying me with food to soften me up." He gave an exaggerated sigh. "What is it?"

"Since your house is empty, we were wondering if the Maxwells could use it while they're here." She turned to Ruthanne. "Ted and Kellie Maxwell are missionaries with our church. Our house is already full with another family passing through, but the Maxwells have a new baby, and it would be nice if they could get away from the chaos."

"No problem." He included Ruthanne in the conversation. "I went to school with Ted, so it's not like they're strangers. I'll have to be sure the house is ready for company, though, if that's okay with you."

"That's fine. We don't have to get back to feed the animals until this evening."

While Mom and Ruthanne continued their animated talk about crafts, Dad turned to Skye. "I'm worried about your sister's car. I don't think it has long to live."

"Well, she wanted that cute little sports car." He laughed. "And whatever Robyn wants, Robyn gets." He explained for Ruthanne. "When she turned twenty-one, she bought her own car, but it's a lemon. We worry about her every time she drives the thing." He spoke to his dad again. "I'll take a look at it this weekend. I suspect it's something in the transmission."

"Excuse me." Ruthanne looked at him with wide eyes. "I didn't know you were a mechanic. Why didn't you tell me?"

He leaned on his forearm, draping the napkin from his fingers. "Because you'd probably have me fixing your old tractor. You've got me doing everything else."

After a bite of lasagna, he was going to share the story about harvesting alpaca beans, but his mom interrupted with a question to Ruthanne. "How is Hannah? Do you think she'll pull through?"

Skye would rather talk about alpaca beans.

Ruthanne swirled her pasta with her fork. "I'm praying she does. The coma is medically induced to help her lungs heal, but the doctor says her recovery afterward could take some time."

Mom reached for Ruthanne's hand. "We've been praying, too, dear."

Ruthanne muttered a thank-you while Mom slid her gaze toward Skye. Did he see accusation there, as if he were supposed to agree to be praying, too? It left as quickly as it had come, but he knew he'd just been reprimanded.

≈

As they entered Skye's house, a charming redbrick bungalow, Ruthanne glanced around with interest. What little she saw from the living room told her volumes about the man who had invaded her sanctuary a week ago.

For a male domain it was surprisingly neat. He probably cleaned up knowing he'd be gone for a month but still. No suspicious dog hair lay in the baseboard crevice, no fingerprints on the television set; the nap of the rug suggested regular vacuuming. Did he hire someone to clean for him? Or maybe his mom had taken the opportunity while he was gone.

"Make yourself at home." He tossed his keys onto a shelf near the door. "Would you like a drink? I have soda." He pointed toward the kitchen.

"No thank you. I'm stuffed from lunch." She wandered farther into the room, taking in the decor. The Wild West seemed to be the theme. A painting of cowboys sitting around a glowing campfire created a peaceful tone for the room. A striking bronze statue of a horse rearing up on its hindquarters adorned the coffee table.

After watering the plants, an assortment of philodendrons and other easy-to-care-for foliage, he slipped into a hallway. "I just want to check the spare bedroom."

For what? It must look like the rest of the house.

A small fireplace, made of the same brick as the exterior, drew her. Atop the dark wood mantel, pictures of Skye's family sat in strategic clusters. The people in them smiled, waved, and struck silly poses in photos taken in all seasons. His sisters all looked like his mother, strawberry blondish hair of various hues and hazel eyes. Skye was definitely the standout with his dark features and blue eyes.

They all seemed happy.

"There's a photo album in the cabinet by the fireplace." Skye startled her as he moved through with an armful of sheets, blankets, and pillows.

"Is there anything I can do to help?"

"No, that's okay. All I have to do is make the bed."

No doubt. The missionaries couldn't have it cleaner if they moved into a five-star hotel.

She pulled out the photo album, an artfully done scrapbook covered in a brown material simulating leather, put together by a loving hand.

After settling herself on the couch, she opened the book to a page titled OUR FIRST CHOSEN, showing pictures of Skye and his new family. The teen's face held a haunted, almost wary look under his shy grin.

She turned the page. Fourteen-year-old Skye with a birthday cake in front of him. The candles' glow on his scowling face broke her heart. She breathed a prayer of thanks that God had put him with such loving people.

As she flipped through the book, she noticed his demeanor change. Tentative smiles began to appear as he held up a baseball award then broader grins during camping trips, Christmas mornings, and. . . What was this? Skye in a choir? What kind of a voice did he have? He must have gotten his talent from Hannie, whose beautiful solo voice ministered during many a Sunday morning.

She grinned as an impish thought formed in her mind. Skye needed to come to church with her next Sunday so he could meet Hannie's friends. . .and so Ruthanne could hear him sing.

"Okay, I'm ready." He popped into the living room, interrupting Ruthanne's scheming.

She closed the album and put it away. "You have a beautiful family."

His face softened. "Yes. God is good."

"All the time." And would he recognize that God has been good to Hannie as well?

On the way to his car, Ruthanne took in the surrounding neighborhood then glanced back at the house. "This is a lovely home. Do you have someone come in to help you keep it up? Or does your mom make you toe the line?" Curious minds and all that.

He chuckled as he shut her door. When he entered the driver's side, he glanced at her, still smiling. "My mom is a great influencer but no. I had to learn to be neat while in the foster system." The grin on his face vanished as the subject moved from his mom, whom he clearly loved, to the foster homes. "Some places were good, the parents fair. But others. . ."

Ruthanne put her hand on his arm. "That's okay. I can hear it in your voice."

He started the ignition. "When I joined my forever family—"

"Forever family?" She quirked her brow.

His chuckle came back. "That's what my folks call it. Silly, I know."

"Not at all. I'm sure it made you feel secure to know that they loved you enough to keep you forever."

He didn't answer, but his serene smile told her more than words ever could.

"Anyway, I'm the neatest of the bunch." He waited at a busy cross street for the light to change. "My sisters don't know what it's like to be walloped for leaving a toy on the floor. I wanted to be sure I stayed with this family, so I did all I could to make Mom and Dad happy."

"Hannie is the neatest person I know. Maybe you got it from her genes."

His face clouded over as it often did when she spoke of her friend. She vowed to press on in the coming days, hoping to weave stories of Hannie's goodness and to fill in the tapestry of her life for this man who had missed the good parts.

"So, where do you have to go?"

She jumped at his abrupt change of subject. Opening her purse, she quickly drew out the list of craft-supply stores. "I have a handful of stores on my list."

They visited each store, with Ruthanne faithfully sticking to her budget. When they were through, they headed for the interstate, stopping at a red light near a little park.

Not wanting this one-on-one time with Skye to end, Ruthanne turned to him. "I can't believe that huge lunch has worn off already. Would you like to get a hot dog and eat it in the park? It's such a beautiful day."

He pulled away from the intersection slowly while eyeing the park then nearly floored it. "No. I have to be getting back."

To what? The animals weren't due for feeding for another hour. What got him so agitated? Had she said something wrong? No. Something else triggered this reaction. She looked back at the empty park, searching for answers, but whatever disturbed him was no longer there.

six

Every Sunday morning Ruthanne fed and watered the animals by herself. Skye's church met earlier than hers, and because he had to travel a half hour to get there, she'd agreed to split the day's duties, she taking the morning and he the evening.

Once she'd finished her chores, she stood in her own kitchen, sipping green tea and looking out toward the main house. A light was on in the kitchen. Perhaps Skye was fixing his breakfast. Who was this man? Good-natured one moment then ready to box with the world the next. Was he there to honor his commitment to a mother he barely knew? Or was he assessing the property at close range with plans to sell it the moment Hannie was no longer in the picture?

She stood for a good five minutes arguing with herself before finally deciding to go over there. All week she had tried to gain courage to ask Skye to church. Why did she hesitate? Could it have been the ride home from Merrick and the strained silence that nearly deafened her? And the ensuing storm clouds in Skye's demeanor the entire week?

Carrying her mug and a plate of cinnamon muffins Paul had made, she tentatively opened Hannie's back door—halfway hoping Skye had already left the kitchen. But no such luck. He sat at the table eating scrambled eggs, drinking coffee, and reading the Sunday comics. She heard his soft chuckle and hoped they'd put him in a better mood.

"Mind if I join you?" She held out the plate, almost as a peace offering. Ruddy rose from the corner of the kitchen to greet her and tried to act as taste tester. She held the plate high, although she doubted that could have deterred the big dog.

"Ruddy, go lay down." Skye deflated all hope, and Ruddy returned to his corner but watched the floor for any errant morsels. "Sorry about that. Have a seat." He motioned to a chair. At least he didn't bite her head off. That was an improvement over yesterday. She eased herself into the chair across from him. He returned to his paper where a one-dimensional Garfield the cat grinned back at her from the paper.

"What have you got planned today?"

"My church starts"—he lowered the newspaper long enough to check his watch—"in an hour. After that I don't know."

Ruthanne took a deep breath. "Would you like to go to church with me this morning?"

This made him lower the paper and stare at her. One would have thought she had asked him to rob a bank. "No obligation, of course," she quickly clarified. "I just thought you might like to visit Hannie's church. See where she worships."

She hopped up to refill his coffee cup and to give him time to think about his answer.

When she sat back down, he'd lowered the paper, but he had a death grip on it. His sky blue eyes grew dark. But then they narrowed. "I'll go to see where *you* worship."

She accepted the challenge. "Fine. Your car or mine?"

His lips twitched as if he enjoyed the game. "Mine."

She held out her hand. "Deal."

As his hand squeezed around hers, pleasant tingles shot up her arm. She pulled away too quickly, bumping his coffee cup.

"Ow!" She swept away the hot liquid that had spilled onto her wrist.

"Are you hurt?" Skye popped out of the chair and had her at the kitchen sink in nearly the same motion. He gently rinsed her hand off in cold water. "Let me look at that."

Ruthanne watched this man—this caring individual, of whom only moments before she had thought the worst—inspect her burn with a tenderness that touched her soul. What guided his ever-changing emotions?

෨

"I don't think it's bad." Skye inspected the burn, marveling at the softness of Ruthanne's fingers in spite of her rough work at the ranch. Reluctant to let her go, he slipped the dish towel from its bar and dabbed around the reddened skin to keep the water from dripping on the floor.

"It wasn't that hot. I think I reacted before I felt it." She slid her arm away and took the towel from his fingers to finish the drying.

Man, she smelled good. They had worked in close quarters in the stalls before, but with the alpaca scent, he never caught how her hair smelled like flowers. Gone was the makeup she'd applied the other day. Good. She didn't need it to cover her natural beauty.

When he realized he was still only a few inches away from her and staring like an adolescent with a crush, he moved back to the table with a dishrag. "What time is church then?" He concentrated on wiping up the small puddle.

"Eleven o'clock." He looked back at her. She regarded him with her head tilted, as if she were trying to figure him out. Well, good luck with that. He hadn't figured himself out since meeting her. One minute she angered him by speaking about his mother, and the next he was falling all over himself trying to please her.

She left to finish getting ready for church while he cleaned his breakfast dishes and then took Ruddy outside. After a quick game of keep-away with a teeth-perforated disk, he clicked the long leash attached to the spike in the ground onto Ruddy's collar. "I hate to do this to you, but you can't be trusted inside." As he walked away, Ruddy raised on his hind legs, straining against the chain, looking like a roan-colored stallion. "Hey, buddy. Go easy, will ya?" Skye checked the spike to be sure it was secure. He had brought Ruddy's doghouse over and placed it under the back deck out of the weather. "You'll be fine. I'll be home soon."

He noticed Ruthanne in Lirit's paddock. The two nuzzled noses, and Ruthanne petted the alpaca's neck while murmuring to her. What kind of girl talk did they share?

❧

"I don't know, Lirit. I can't figure him out. At times it's as if he's only doing this through some odd sense of obligation. At others he seems so eager to learn."

Lirit flattened her ears and emoted a disgusted grunt that made her lips flap.

"Why don't you like him?" Ruthanne had heard of animals with a special sense toward humans. Did Lirit know something about Skye that he hadn't revealed to Ruthanne? Was he the land-grabbing monster she had painted earlier?

But he was a Christian. And he took care of her coffee-drenched hand. And he smelled so good. It was all she could do to keep from leaning in and taking a big whiff as he tended her wrist. Something woodsy. Not what you'd expect a businessman to wear. And certainly not what Paul wore. Sometimes he was so drenched in cologne she could hardly breathe. She remembered Hannie admonishing him once. She railed on him for ten minutes about how his cologne probably killed hundreds of animals in the testing phase. Then she moved on to what the chemicals were doing to his body. Hannie never wore perfume. Nothing with chemicals ever touched her skin.

And yet she still ended up in the hospital.

"I'm ready." Skye's voice from the side of the house startled her. With one last pat to Lirit's neck, she tugged the strap of her woven purse tighter to her shoulder and joined him.

❧

As they made their way to the garage, Skye saw Ruthanne

dart a shy glance toward him. He had to resist the urge to put his arm around her.

"You look nice." He meant it this time. Even though her pink skirt had a strong gypsy influence with the billowy top, it didn't scream hippie like her other choice of clothing.

"You, too. But you don't need to wear a tie."

He glanced down at the tie his mother had given him for his fortieth birthday. The color of his eyes. He didn't know what came over him when he chose to wear the tie that morning. He never wore one to his own church. "You want me to take it off?" He started to loosen the knot.

"No. It looks good." A blush dusted her cheeks. Yep, that's why he'd chosen the tie.

They reached his car parked in the drive. He opened her door for her, but before she slipped inside, she grabbed the door frame. "Skye, Paul is taking me to see Hannie right after church. They did a tracheal intubation on her yesterday."

"I know. He called to tell me."

"I'm anxious to see her without her face obstructed. Although I'm not sure I can handle a tube in her throat." Her large eyes searched his. "Would you join us?"

He agreed, sensing that she was asking for herself this time. But an excuse hovered just inside his lips, ready to rescue him.

Fifteen minutes later Ruthanne instructed him to pull into the parking lot of Faith Community Church, a small building probably built in the 1960s. The roof slanted in a long slope, and the windows were in a geometric pattern.

Just inside the small foyer, Paul stood talking to a woman. About food, of course.

The ample middle-aged woman clung to Paul's elbow. "I didn't expect you to take on the whole party. I'll bring the teas though."

"That's good, because I know food, but tea is a woman's domain."

The henlike woman reached out for Ruthanne, and Skye trailed behind her.

"What a gem you have found in this man. I hope you plan on keeping him."

Ruthanne's half grin didn't suggest a woman in love.

Paul stepped in. "Hey, Ruthie and I are just good friends." He draped his arm over her shoulders.

Good friends? All Skye had witnessed since moving in was Paul's attention toward Ruthanne. He told himself to keep his distance until he assessed the playing field more thoroughly.

The woman finished her conversation with Paul and bustled into the sanctuary.

Paul noticed Skye and shook his hand. "Hey, glad you could make it. Ruthanne called me to say you were coming." He looked down at her. "I notified the girls."

Her hand flew to her open mouth. "You didn't!"

Skye looked at Ruthanne and then at Paul. "The girls?"

Ruthanne's gaze darted around the foyer as she placed her hand on Skye's arm. "Four of Hannie's friends. They are remarkable artisans and have sort of formed a club with Hannie as their leader."

"What? Like the Ya-Ya Crafthood?"

"Something like that. They're all about the same age and—"

"There he is!"

Skye turned at the sound of a woman fast approaching him, her sandaled feet slapping the tiled floor. Short, burgundy hair adorned her head, and she seemed weighted down with the turquoise jewelry around her neck and on each finger. Three other women trailed after her like naturally graying tails on a brightly colored kite.

Oh great! Granola-fueled earth mothers.

Ruthanne tried to step between Skye and the women, but they sailed past her.

"Look at his eyes. Just like his mother's." Skye felt like a museum piece as they scrutinized him. He wished he'd had a corded rope surrounding him to keep them from touching.

Each woman had been a hippie in her day. He could tell by their natural-fiber clothing, the long, uncut hair of the trailing three, and the telltale wrinkles around their mouths from drawing on too many homemade marijuana cigarettes.

He wanted to hurl. Any one of them could have been in the commune when he was little.

Ruthanne made the introductions. "Skye, this is Lark, Daisy, Saffron, and Agnes."

Agnes?

She must have tried to break out of the stereotype. Agnes had led the pack. She slipped her long, bony fingers around his bicep. "We're all praying for Hannie. She's one special lady."

"So I've heard." His brusque response convicted him, and he softened when he saw how deeply these women loved his mother. He covered her hand at his elbow. "Thank you."

Through a shimmer of tears, Lark glanced toward the open door of the sanctuary. "The music has started. Please, if you need anything, let us know."

Skye nodded, and the four flower children left him the same way they had arrived. Nonconformists. They all looked alike, so what was the point? But these women had good hearts, and they obviously loved the Lord.

Ruthanne drew him into the sanctuary. Only then did he hear the music. As they made their way to the chairs, she leaned toward him to speak. "I'm sorry about Hannie's friends. Paul shouldn't have told them you were coming."

He glanced to Paul, who was clapping and singing on the other side of Ruthanne. "It's okay. That's why I'm here, right? To learn about my mother?"

Ruthanne offered a sad smile but didn't say anything. She briefly squeezed his arm. From that moment on, Skye had a hard time concentrating on the service.

%

During the praise music Skye never opened his mouth. Now how was Ruthanne supposed to compare his voice to Hannie's if he didn't cooperate?

The music finished, leaving her feeling in a less than worshipful mood. She had concentrated too much on Skye and not enough on the Lord. But when the pastor announced prayer time, Ruthanne began to feel the gentle pull of the Holy Spirit.

"We have so many needs in our body today," the pastor spoke. "Let's turn to our neighbors and take a moment to pray for each other."

People began whispering their requests to each other, the soft voices like a straw broom whisking away debris. Paul turned to Ruthanne. Normally she relished their prayer time together. But today she whispered that she wanted to pray with Skye. He tipped his head slightly in resigned agreement and instead of joining her turned to the person on his right.

She took Skye's hand, and his eyes widened in surprise. "Please pray for Hannie with me."

He winced as if Hannie's name had become a hot poker. But he allowed her to take the other hand, and standing there together, they bowed their heads. Ruthanne uttered a heartfelt prayer, one she'd prayed often since Hannie's illness. But then she prayed for Skye.

"Lord, I pray for peace for Skye. This hasn't been easy for him. I can't imagine the emotions he's had to deal with since learning about his mother. He may someday have some decisions to make—" Her throat caught. Silently she prayed she wouldn't cry. Those decisions could affect her adversely, but she didn't want this to be a selfish prayer. "Tough decisions that I trust You'll guide him through. Above all, I pray You help him to smile more. . . ." She let the last request trail off, realizing she was about say, *as that would be an indication that You're working in his life.* But she didn't know him well enough to be so bold.

When she looked up at the end of her prayer, he was gazing at her. No storm clouds in those eyes. They seemed brighter, as if unshed tears purified their color.

"Thank you." He pressed her hand to his chest. How long they stood there together, she had no way of knowing. But eventually the pastor's voice pulled her back.

&

Skye tore his gaze from Ruthanne and noticed Paul glancing toward them, his eyes darting to their clasped hands. He reluctantly let go. Did Paul think their behavior inappropriate, or did he indeed have feelings for Ruthanne?

Skye only knew that after his mother's friends had assaulted him, he had decided he would make yet another excuse to avoid seeing his mother. But an incredible strength surged through him as Ruthanne prayed.

As long as she was there, he could enter that hospital room.

seven

Skye's shoes squeaked on the freshly buffed floor as he followed Ruthanne and Paul down the corridor. The closer he came to his mother's room, the more he wanted out. Ruthanne glanced over her shoulder and smiled at him.

He took a deep breath. He could do this. As long as she continued to gift him with that sweet smile, he would be strong.

They entered the room, and the other two walked to either side of the bed. Skye hung back, his shoulders pressed into the doorjamb—one foot in, one foot out. So much for staying strong.

His mother lay in exactly the same position as the first time he'd seen her. But she looked different with the respirator mask off. Even with her face exposed, she was still not the mother he remembered.

Ruthanne leaned down and spoke softly. "Hannie, we're here." She took a comb from her purse and began grooming the woman. "Honestly, Hannie, you don't move an inch, yet your hair is always mussed when I come in."

Paul followed suit. "Hey, Auntie. Brought you a tofu burger."

Ruthanne looked at him in surprise. "Now what would you do if she woke up and wanted it?"

"I'd go make her one." Paul began rubbing the frail arms and legs. He spoke to Skye. "This helps keep the circulation going."

Skye nodded. The lump in his throat refused to budge. Watching these two dote on his mother stirred an emotion Skye never thought he'd have: jealousy. It rose up from his bowels, clinging to every nerve ending on the way up. This was *his* mother, a woman he barely knew yet she'd made room for two strangers in her life. No, more than that. She'd made room for an entire community.

A voice in his head, clearly not God's but impossible to silence, challenged his thoughts like a bully on a playground. *Look at these two people. She loved them far more than she ever loved you.* Skye squeezed his fists into his eyes to shut out the scene before him. *You were worthless. Just something that needed to be fed.* His heart bled from a tangible wound as the bully struck his final blow. *She never loved you. You were a tumor that she couldn't wait to get rid of after your father died.*

He bounded out of the hospital room, nearly spilling a metal meal cart, his chest about to implode. Hot tears burned his eyes like acid.

Somehow he managed to navigate the halls out to the parking lot. Good thing Paul had chosen to take his own car to the hospital after church. Ruthanne had a way home.

A mist fell that chilled him to the core. He climbed into his car and shot an angry glance upward through the windshield toward the sky—his namesake. The hippie name once sickened him. His mother often told him the sky was his father, and he had his eyes. Whenever he was in trouble, he should look up. Father Sky would solve his problems.

Skye ground the gears and tore out of the parking lot. Down the road, a traffic light suddenly turned yellow. He skidded to a stop. Only then did he realize he'd been going twenty miles over the speed limit.

Gray clouds hung heavy behind the red traffic light. Another voice entered his swirling thoughts—that of the woman who raised him. His spiritual anchor, Mom. *It's okay to look to the sky, but remember, you'll only get your answers from the One who created it.* He clenched the steering wheel. The other voice drowned out that reason. *If your mother lived so close, why didn't she try to find you earlier? What made her do it now? Guilt? The fear of dying?* With one foot on the clutch, he revved the engine until the light turned green. When it changed, his foot bore down on the gas pedal.

Just out of Oakley, the two-lane highway opened before him, and he took the curves like a Grand Prix veteran. His accuser's voice clung to the back bumper. *What game is she playing now? If she got her life together, why didn't she find you when you grew up? What does she want from you?* Skye couldn't go fast enough to shake it. A couple of miles later he swerved onto the road leading to the ranch.

Mom had told him: *Remember that Hannah is a person, too. She deserves prayers as much as anyone else. I hope you've been lifting her before the Lord.*

Conflicting memories sparred within. He sped past the few homes dotting the valley. The ranch suddenly came into view, his preoccupation nearly causing him to sail on past.

Then—

A flash of red fur.

He fought the steering wheel as he veered left.

Slick mud marked for landscaping.

The barn.

Wood cracked and splintered.

The car finally stopped in an SUV-sized hole. The air bag, a rough, powdery marshmallow, punched his face and slammed his head into the headrest. An acrid smell assaulted his nose.

Disoriented, he opened the door and slid out. A sharp pain jabbed in the arch of his right foot. He stumbled, twisting his ankle, and fell to the cement floor on his left shoulder. Agony sliced through his body.

He lay there on his back, praying the whole thing had just been a nasty dream. He rolled away from the car, but—

Knifing pain.

Blessed darkness.

Squawking chickens brought him back—probably only moments later—encircling him in a feathered frenzy. From his supine position, he could see long-haired rabbits springing among the poultry.

What had he done?

"Skye!"

Ruthanne's voice. Outside. She must not have been far behind him. He tried to get up, but his arm wouldn't work. Her voice grew nearer. He wished he could crawl away. Disappear. Never be seen again.

"Skye?" She was in the barn, but he didn't call out to her. His own voice accused him. *Stupid!* He closed his eyes.

Her trembling hands gently inspected his face and chest. "Oh no. Skye! Please, God, no!"

"Go away."

The hands lifted off him. "What?"

"I'm an idiot and don't deserve any medical attention."

Tender hands touched his cheeks. He opened his eyes, fearing what he'd see there. Ruthanne's face showed nothing but concern. A siren sounded in the distance, and he groaned. His car's emergency system must have alerted the paramedics when his air bag went off. He squeezed his eyes shut again.

"Skye!" She grabbed him by his shirt. "Stay with me." Was she going to slap him?

"I'm not unconscious. Just embarrassed."

He opened his eyes again to see her kneeling, elbows akimbo as she leaned her hands on her hips. "What happened?"

"I guess I was going too fast when I pulled in the drive, and something red came out of nowhere." His breath caught in his throat. "It was Ruddy!"

Her sad eyes frightened him. "Yes, it was Ruddy."

He tried to sit up again, but she pressed him back down. "He's okay. You must have clipped him though. He's favoring his back leg. When we pulled up, we saw him slinking toward the front porch. He's probably trying to escape punishment."

"I've got to find him." He tried to sit up, but the pain caused a buzzing in his ears.

She placed her hand on his chest. "Paul ran to catch him before he could take off. He'll be fine. We'll have our vet look at him."

"Now."

"Soon. First we need to get you to the hospital."

Not the hospital! He didn't want to go back there where it all started.

He had no choice. The rescue unit arrived and loaded him into the ambulance.

~

"I'm glad we left the hospital not long after him. He must have just landed in the barn when we got there." Ruthanne paced the emergency waiting room while Paul sat in a chair. She rubbed her arms and muttered, more to herself than to Paul. "Why did he run? What is it about Hannie that scares him?"

Paul shook his head. "Not a clue. Have you asked him?"

She stopped pacing and looked at him. "It's not really my business, is it?"

"It might be now. He's caused a mess out at your place, all because of this thing with Aunt Hannie."

Ruthanne sank into the chair beside Paul. "You're her nephew. Why don't you talk to Skye? You *are* family."

Paul frowned. "I don't think he'd tell me. We're not exactly friends."

"You're probably right. All we can do is pray." Ruthanne sighed and looked at the clock. Skye had only been in there a half hour.

The glass door opened, and Skye's parents rushed in. Mrs. Randall's face was full of concern. She spotted Ruthanne and nearly ran into her arms.

"He's okay." Ruthanne could barely get the words out as

the woman squeezed her neck like a boa constrictor. "Just banged up a little."

Mrs. Randall relaxed. "I know, but a mother imagines all kinds of things. Thank you for calling us." She pressed a tissue to her chest with one hand and held her husband's hand with the other.

Paul stood, and Ruthanne made the introductions.

"I'm sure he'll be out soon." Ruthanne pulled Mrs. Randall to a black plastic chair and sat down beside her.

Mrs. Randall drew a deep breath. As the color returned to her face, she turned to Paul. "How long have you known Skye's birth mother?"

"She married my uncle when I was twelve. We all love her."

Ruthanne noticed the older woman's lips pinch into two cranberry lines. Was this as hard on her as it was on Skye? What did she know about Hannie's early life?

Before she lost her nerve, Ruthanne posed the question she wished she could ask Skye. "Do you know what happened to Skye when he lived with Hannie?"

His parents cast sidelong glances at each other. Mrs. Randall answered. "Not all of it. Only what has come out gradually."

"Do you know why Hannie put him up for adoption?"

They both shifted in their seats. Her questions were having an uncomfortable effect on them.

"Did he tell you she did that?"

Mr. Randall's question took her aback. They acted as if there were another alternative. "Well, no. He hasn't said anything about his mother."

Skye's dad leaned forward with his elbows on his knees, pinning Ruthanne with a firm yet compassionate gaze. "We're not at liberty to discuss Skye's affairs since he hasn't given us permission for that. I'm sure, if you continue your friendship with him, much will come to light."

"We have prayed together often for his birth mother," Mrs.

Randall said. "I'm pleased that she found such loving people to finally settle down with."

Finally? Ruthanne felt an odd, queasy feeling in the pit of her stomach. Her husband had been a rover. He never "finally" settled anywhere. Had Hannie been like Brian at one time? Could that have been why she held such empathy for him?

Hannie, what kind of a mother were you?

Just then Skye hobbled into the room, with his left arm in a large sling and a crutch under the other. Abrasions across the bridge of his nose indicated where the air bag had made contact. He was lucky nothing had been broken.

His mother gasped and rushed toward him.

"I'm fine." His words had no effect as she began inspecting him for further wounds. "They gave me a tetanus shot because I stepped on a nail sticking out of a board when I got out of my car. The nail caused me to sprain my ankle. Not bad but the doctor said it will be sore for a week or two. But because of the sudden pain from my ankle, I fell onto my shoulder. It's dislocated." He smiled weakly at his mother. "No other injuries, I promise."

"I'm sure you're sore all over just from the impact."

"Yeah. There is that."

His father touched his good shoulder. "We'll take you to our house since the missionaries are in yours."

"No." Skye looked past his father at Ruthanne. "I have an obligation and now a mess to clean up. I'll stay at the ranch."

Ruthanne had mixed feelings about that. The more she became acquainted with the man, the more she liked being with him. However, what could he do to help now? "Skye, you can go home and heal then continue your thirty days."

By the set of his jaw, she could tell he'd made up his mind.

"Fine." She raised her hands in resignation. "I'll take you home."

In her car he asked about Ruddy.

"Paul left him with my vet before coming to the hospital. I'm sure he's okay."

He stared out the passenger-side window. "Let's swing by there."

"Skye—"

"Please." He turned his gaze on her. She knew the pain she saw there was greater than his physical discomfort.

"Okay." She took the next left instead of going straight.

At the veterinarian's office Ruddy sat in a large cage, whining and wagging his tail so hard it beat a rhythm on the plastic sides.

Skye shuffled to the cage and gingerly knelt down. "I'm sorry, buddy. I didn't see you until it was too late." He looked up at Ruthanne. "He must have been frightened by the thunder. That's the only reason he would have escaped his collar and run around to the front of the house."

Poor Ruddy had a cast on his right back leg. Ironic, since his master had his right foot bandaged.

The pair made quite a sight as Ruthanne loaded them both into her small car. Ruddy filled the backseat, where he licked the back of Skye's neck.

Ruthanne had to laugh. "Looks like there are no hard feelings."

Skye managed to reach behind his head to pet the dog. "Either that or he's trying to get on my good side so I won't punish him for leaving the backyard."

When they pulled into the driveway, Ruthanne forced herself not to cry. The tow truck had come for Skye's car, and the gaping hole in the barn was bigger than she'd thought.

"Ruthanne, I'm so sorry. My insurance will pay for the damage, and I'll do what I can to make it as good as new."

She opened the driver's side door. "We'll talk about it later. Right now let's get you and your dog inside and comfortable."

●

eight

Ruthanne felt compassion for Skye as he tried to help Ruddy into the house. She didn't know which one hobbled the worst. As she opened the door, the delicious aroma of succulent beef stew greeted her. She rushed through the house and found Paul in the kitchen, a wooden spoon in his hand. A warm feeling settled into her weary bones. "You didn't have to do this, you know."

Paul looked up and grinned. "I was going to take you out to dinner tonight but figured this would work out better. I had the stew in the freezer."

She walked over to him and stood on tiptoes to place a kiss on his temple. "Thank you."

When she turned, Skye and Ruddy were in the doorway. Skye seemed to avoid eye contact. "I'm not hungry. I think I'll go to my room."

Ruthanne scurried to his side. "Let me help you up the stairs."

"The stairs." He drooped his head. With a glance at the crutch under his right arm and the sling holding his left shoulder, Ruthanne knew he was calculating just how he was going to maneuver the staircase.

"Uh-oh. The handrail is on the wrong side, isn't it?"

Paul had stopped stirring the stew and was now slicing artisan bread into hearty slices. "I could carry you, old man." Was he serious or not? Ruthanne couldn't tell.

"No thank you," Skye nearly growled at him.

Ruthanne took the crutch and slipped under Skye's arm then guided him to the sofa in the living room. When his leg was propped and a pillow supported his arm, she handed him the television remote. Ruddy settled on the floor near his master, and Ruthanne promised him a special doggy treat for his faithfulness.

With hands on her hips, she looked at Skye. "Now, you will rest here, and when supper is ready, I'll bring it out to you."

Skye started to protest, but Ruthanne held up her hand. "I've spoken my piece." Then she turned and headed back to the kitchen.

➤

"I've spoken my piece." Skye chuckled under his breath as he watched her retreating figure. She sure looked cute trying to tell him what to do.

But then he remembered walking in and seeing her kiss Paul.

Skye mentally kicked himself. What was he doing, falling for someone who already had a great guy? And worse, someone who was dedicated to the woman who ruined his childhood?

Frustrated by his mixed emotions, he turned on the television and found a Seattle Mariners baseball game.

➤

While Paul prepared their dinner, Ruthanne slipped out to tend the animals. When she was through, she leaned against Lirit's paddock, placing her foot on the bottom rail. The two nuzzled noses while Ruthanne stroked the long neck, praying, "Lord, I don't know why You've brought that man here. He's been nothing but trouble. And now he's put a hole in the barn."

Tom, their part-time handyman, was due back tomorrow— and not a moment too soon. Skye said he'd fix everything, but it was a mystery as to how he would manage that feat.

After a good-night hug for Lirit, Ruthanne went back into the house where Paul had joined Skye. The two rivals now cheered for the same team. Paul had brought out Skye's supper and was just finishing his own. Ruddy had a bowl on the floor, licked spotless.

She moved into their line of vision since neither had acknowledged her presence. With her arms folded, she looked at both of them. "You could have waited."

Skye slurped the last of the gravy from his spoon. "Couldn't. It smelled too good."

It did smell good. She offered to bring Skye seconds and filled her own bowl.

When the game ended, Ruthanne walked Paul to the front porch where she thanked him once more for the stew. "You're always there for me. What a great friend you are."

Paul's eyes dimmed. "Friend?"

Ruthanne kissed his cheek. "A wonderful friend. You were there when Brian left me. And when word came that he'd died, you walked me through it, gave advice, prayed. And you keep taking care of me."

There was a time when they dated briefly that she wanted to love Paul. However, eventually she had known he could only be a brother to her.

A slight breeze blew a tuft of hair over his forehead, and she reached up to move it back. "Go home, Paul. I'll see you tomorrow."

He nodded, offering a tiny smile, then slipped his hands into his pockets and whistled while he strolled to his car.

Ruthanne shook her head. Until the day he found his true love, he would keep trying.

She went back inside to find Skye fighting sleep. Kneeling down next to him, she spoke barely above a whisper. "Do you need anything? A pain pill?"

"No, I just took one, and that's why I'm groggy." He grinned at her as he sank further into his pillow. "Thanks for putting up with me. I promise I'll make it up to you."

"We'll talk about that later. I know you don't want to try

the stairs. Would you like to sleep in Hannie's room tonight? There are fresh sheets on the bed."

His eyes widened, and a look of terror replaced the silly drug-induced smile. "No! I can't go in there."

Can't?

"Okay, you can sleep on the couch tonight." He relaxed, and she watched him fall asleep. As much as she loved Hannie, she couldn't push aside the fact that her son was afraid of her.

She moved a stray wisp of hair from his forehead the same way she had with Paul. But different feelings stirred within her. Protectiveness, yes. She wanted to fix whatever bothered him. But something else, too. She closed her eyes to remember how their day had started. Yes. Those feelings were there when they'd prayed together at church.

His arm felt cool, so she rose and found a blanket. He didn't even stir as she gently laid it over him. Emotions played ping-pong in her heart. Was this man her enemy? Or would he turn out to be the one to heal her heart after Brian had torn it to shreds?

She left before the temptation to kiss his lips grew too strong.

Early the next day, Ruthanne rose to feed the animals. When she entered the barn to retrieve the wheelbarrow, she noticed Skye struggling with it. The crutch lay on the ground, and his left arm had escaped the sling. But what alarmed her was that he had somehow managed to load the large feed bag. He made a pitiful picture with his injured foot barely touching the ground and his bad shoulder drooped to reduce the stress.

"Oh for goodness' sake," she muttered as she ran to help him. "What do you think you're doing?" With a light push, she nudged him out of the way and grabbed the handles of the wheelbarrow.

"My chores."

"The alpacas will starve before you get this over to them. How did you manage to load a forty-pound bag?"

"I tipped the wheelbarrow on its side, knelt down so I wouldn't put pressure on my foot, then scooped the bag into it with my good arm."

"I'm impressed by your ingenuity, but you didn't plan the rest of the execution very well, did you?"

He stroked his chin. "Guess it's back to the drawing board, huh?" He grinned, and Ruthanne suddenly remembered how she had almost kissed those lips just the night before.

"I'll make you a deal." She began wheeling out the door. "Let me feed the animals until you can maneuver better. We'll find light duty for you until you heal."

He hesitated as if he were about to argue. But after regarding the crutch still on the ground, he sighed. "You're right." He hopped the few feet to pick it up then slowly gimped his way out of the barn. "Sorry."

"Skye."

He turned back to look at her.

Ruthanne placed her hands on her hips. "If you keep asking for forgiveness, I may have to rescind it."

If it were possible for sad eyes to twinkle, his did. "Yes, Boss Lady."

Ruthanne finished feeding and watering the alpacas. In the process she checked on the pregnant females, watching for any change in their behavior.

When she finished, she heard pounding coming from the barn. Skye stood at the workbench, making a new door for the rabbit pen.

"Where did you get the wood?" She inspected it and found he'd done a decent job.

"I took a board from inside the wall that I smashed through. I was gathering all the debris and saw some boards that could be trimmed and used for other things."

"Nothing's wasted?" She tilted her head, trying to get a good view of his face.

"Nothing." He smiled back.

"What happened here?" a male voice bellowed from outside.

Ruthanne looked toward the source. "Tom's back."

❧

Skye watched a large shadow form just outside the hole in the barn. He imagined a hefty, snarling wrestler ready to tear him apart for creating such a mess. "Who's Tom?"

"Our handyman."

A knot formed in Skye's throat. If that shadow were any indication of the guy's size, he was really in for it.

Ruthanne cupped her mouth. "We're in here, Tom."

Snitch.

The man stepped through the jagged cavity rather than using the door. Although not the monster Skye had imagined, Tom was still tall but portly and seemed to be somewhere in his sixties. He wore jeans, a Western-style plaid shirt, and sported a receding rusty gray hairline and a long ponytail.

Ruthanne gave him a brief hug. "How was Colorado?"

Tom couldn't seem to take his eyes off the hole. "It was fine." He dragged his gaze toward Ruthanne. Skye stood behind her, where Tom noticed him for the first time. "Who's this?"

"I'm sorry. Where are my manners?" Ruthanne pointed toward Skye. "This is Skye Randall, Hannie's son. You know she asked for him when she became ill."

"Yes, I knew." Tom's demeanor changed, and he peered into Skye's eyes as if trying to see what was inside his head.

"And this is Tom," Ruthanne finished the introduction. "A dear friend and the best all-around fixer-upper in southern Oregon. He's just been to Colorado for his daughter's wedding."

Skye held out his hand and felt the raw power in Tom's meaty grip.

"I didn't want to leave with Hannie so sick, but Ruthanne insisted."

"Hannie would have insisted." She patted his arm and filled him in on Hannie's condition.

"Now what happened here?" Tom pointed to the gash in the barn.

"I happened here." Skye swallowed the lame excuse that leaped to his lips.

"Excuse me?"

"I drove my car into the wall."

If Tom's shadow seemed fierce, the man himself suddenly embodied the wrestler of Skye's imagination. "Were you drinking, boy?"

Skye jumped to attention. "No, sir. It had been raining, and I hit a slick patch when I swerved to avoid my dog."

"I saw the tracks in my landscaping. I was going to get to it when I got back." The way Tom glared at him, with one eye nearly shut, reminded Skye of someone. But he couldn't remember who.

Tom turned his gaze to Ruthanne. "He telling the truth?"

She nodded. "I've never seen Skye drink. He's a Christian."

The wrestler suddenly turned into a large teddy bear. "That's great!"

Was that a tear in the man's eye? What was wrong with this guy?

Tom grabbed Skye's hand and pulled him into a one-armed hug.

Skye extracted himself and tried to bring the conversation to the more practical matter at hand. "I plan to fix this mess I made."

Tom looked at Skye's shoulder then at the crutch under his arm. "How you going to do that?"

"I don't know. But I'm not the kind of person who runs from my responsibilities." Not like his mother.

Tom nodded as if approving that statement. "We'll fix it together."

Now Skye nodded his approval. "I'd like that."

৵

That night Skye's ankle, although still extremely sore, felt well enough for him to navigate the stairs. Ruddy followed him up, limping on his own bum leg.

After a long, hot shower with the water running on his aching arm, Skye slipped into bed. Normally at peak condition, he found dealing with a sling and crutch more tiring than mucking out paddocks.

In his sleep he dreamed of a party, and judging by the size of the people, he was a child. Loud music played, the kind that hurt your ears no matter how it loud it was. He wandered through the crowd of people, and none of them knew he was there. He might just as well be a stray dog. He wanted Mommy but couldn't find her. Suddenly strong hands grabbed him, and he heard a scream. A woman's scream.

Skye woke up startled, thankful the dream was over. But then he heard the scream again. He sat straight up as Ruddy barked softly from his bed on the floor. Then several women screamed.

He shot out of bed despite his injuries, pulled on his jeans, and tore open the balcony door. Forgetting about his crutch, he launched down the deck steps, favoring his sore ankle. The partial moon above illuminated Ruthanne in the back pasture. She held a rifle to her shoulder with something sighted through the scope. Limping out to her, he called her name so she wouldn't shoot him. She never even twitched. What was the woman doing with a rifle? Was that her screaming? Where were the other women he heard?

"Are you okay?" His labored breathing caused sharp pains in his shoulder.

The rifle continued to track something out in the darkness.

She trailed it through the scope. "I'm fine. Why do you ask?"

"Why do I ask?" He grabbed the rifle barrel and lowered it. She glared at him with annoyance. "I heard a woman scream. I thought it was you until I heard several."

Her eyes turned back to the darkness. "Ooh! There he is." She lifted the gun again. *Pop!* "Missed him."

"Is it a wolf?" Skye squinted, thinking he saw something canine darting around in the brush.

"No, just the neighbor's dog. He has a habit of stalking our alpacas, and I haven't been able to convince his owners."

"Are you trying to kill him?" Skye couldn't believe that Ruthanne would harm an animal. But then again, she was mighty fierce when it came to her alpacas.

"I got you now. . . ." Her voice had dropped to a whisper. *Pop!*

The large black lab yelped and ran away with a luminescent yellow splotch on its side.

Skye grabbed the rifle to inspect it. "A paint gun?"

"I thought if I could tag him somehow, I'd have evidence that it was him. Tomorrow I'll go over there and explain why their dog is in Technicolor now."

Was it the stress of dredging up the past? Or the pain in his body? Or maybe the fact that he was falling for this wild, wonderful woman? Skye didn't know. But waves of laughter poured from him, and he sank to the hard ground holding his left arm.

She flopped down to join him, her infectious giggle only making things worse.

"So what was the screaming about?" he finally managed to ask.

"Oh." She wiped her eyes. "That's how alpacas sound when they're frightened."

"No kidding?"

"No kidding."

This only got them started again. When the laughter finally

died down, Skye said, "You do realize we're on the ground in the middle of the night and laughing like fools."

Another giggle struggled to escape her throat. "Oh really? I hadn't noticed." The giggle bubbled out of her, and Skye realized he'd have to be the strong one. Her week had been just as hard as his emotionally. And judging by her near hysterical laughter, she obviously needed some good REM sleep.

He nudged her shoulder. "Come on, Deadeye. You look great, but I need my beauty rest." When he realized he had no crutch to help him stand, he looked at her helplessly.

"Allow me." Ruthanne stood, reached out her hand, and hauled him to his feet.

They were now only inches from each other, still holding each other's hands. The moon overhead cast a velvet glow over her beautiful face, which was upturned and, oh, so inviting.

"Deadeye, eh?" She tilted her head. "What does that mean?"

He pulled her even closer, pleased that she hadn't let go of him either.

"In old Westerns, that was always the guy who never missed a shot."

Her mouth twitched. "I think I'd rather be called Calamity Jane. At least it sounds more feminine."

"Calamity it is then." And he leaned down and kissed her.

nine

The next morning Ruthanne shook her head. "What is he doing now?"

Skye acted like he didn't still have his arm in a sling or a crutch under his arm. Ruthanne found him in the pasture with the four-wheeled wagon and a shovel. At least he'd given up on using the wheelbarrow.

"You are absolutely the most stubborn patient I've ever seen."

"The least I can do until Tom gets here is clean up poop." With his jaw jutted forward and lips pressed into a determined line, he struggled one-handed with the shovel. He slipped the blade underneath the communal pile, trying not to get too many beans so he could lift and toss them into the wagon. Even so, some of the beans escaped on the ride to the wagon and rolled down the short hill. Every time he lifted the shovel, he'd lose some beans. Three young male alpacas found the skittering-beans game a delight and chased them down the hill, kicking at them and inspecting the marble-sized balls with floppy lips.

"Skye."

"What?"

"Let me do that."

"No."

"You're going to hurt yourself."

He stabbed the shovel into the ground and leaned his wrist on the handle. "I will not be the first man in history to have an alpaca poop-shoveling injury. How would I explain *that* to my insurance company?" Bent on finishing the job, he continued the awkward chore.

If a man could be attractive doing this menial job—with a handicap—Skye pulled it off to perfection. She thought about the kiss they'd shared the night before. Actually she hadn't stopped thinking about the kiss. Such a tender man shouldn't have to face the emotional pain he always seemed to carry.

A God-inspired thought entered her head. Knowing he wasn't ready to talk about Hannie, Ruthanne decided to slay two Goliath-sized problems with one stone. She let him struggle a few moments more until she could tell by the luster of sweat above his upper lip that he was nearly done.

"Skye, I've been thinking about the craft fair." She launched her plan. "Without Hannie to organize, I'm thinking of pulling out." She paused to gauge his emotions. "But we've already paid the fee."

Money seemed to light a spark. "And they won't refund it?"

"Not at this late date." She tried to look as forlorn as she could without tipping her hand.

"What needs to be done?"

"Hannie had planned to sell some of her weavings. A small paddock will be set up for a couple of alpacas, too. Paul will be there, but I'll need an extra person to man the cash register while I do the demonstration."

"I can do that."

She had no doubt he would agree to helping at the fair. But her next request required a move from God. "Great. Would you like to help me choose some weavings to put on display? They're all in the shop in the walk-out basement." He had never been in the shop, avoiding it with one excuse or another. She watched storm clouds form in his sky blue eyes, signaling yet another refusal. She'd hoped by presenting the request in a way that would help her out of a predicament, he'd overcome whatever was keeping him from getting near his mother.

Her sneaky approach seemed to work. He finally agreed, weak and somewhat breathless. "Okay."

He allowed her to finish shoveling the pile. As she reached for the wagon handle, he brushed her aside. "I can pull it."

"How?"

"See this rope?" He grasped a rope tied to the handle.

"I saw it, but I don't know why it's there."

He tied the other end around his waist and, leaning on his crutch, held out his arm in a half ta-da pose.

"You are determined, aren't you?" Ruthanne shook her head as they walked together. "Sick but determined."

Once they deposited the contents of their wagon onto the compost pile, they headed back to the house. In the cool shadow under the deck, Ruthanne unlocked the door to the shop, realizing it had been too long since she'd been in there.

With a flick of the light switch, colors, textures, and patterns greeted her like old friends. "I apologize for the mustiness. Maybe I should open this place up every day."

Skye stuck his head in the door, as if he weren't sure what evil might await him inside the room. Finally he walked to a wall displaying several hangings. "My mother did all of these?"

Ruthanne nodded. "She spins the yarn then creates these beautiful masterpieces."

His eyes darted over the rest of the artwork in the room. "How lucrative is this business?"

"You'd be surprised what the Internet brings in." She held up a palm-sized alpaca. "These toys were made by the people she visits. It's great therapy, and 100 percent profit goes into her ministry fund. Among the people represented in this bin alone, more than half accepted Christ while working on these toys."

He raised an eyebrow, but a small grin played on his face.

"Impressive." He inspected the fuzzy toy then put it back in the bin.

After a quick glance around the room, Ruthanne spotted where she wanted to start.

❧

Skye prayed for strength as Ruthanne walked over to a wall where a weaving the size of a small throw rug hung. His mother had touched every piece of art in there. Other than her bedroom, this was her most personal space in the house.

"This is my favorite." Ruthanne glowed with pride as she pointed out the striking two-foot by three-foot woven cloth featuring a butterfly. "This one isn't for sale. She made it for me, and I keep it here to showcase for our visitors. Notice how she contrasted the dark with the light—black background but vibrant shades of orange and yellow for the large monarch in the middle."

Ruthanne stroked a wing with the back of her finger. "This is me." Then she indicated the dark background. "And this is where I was when I first met Hannie. See the leaves that the butterfly is sitting on?"

He looked closer. The two green leaves were in reality two hands holding the butterfly in their palm.

"Hannie told me this is God. I also like to think of the two hands as Hannie and David. God used these two people to lift me up and give me wings."

Ruthanne's eyes shimmered with unshed tears. He caressed her shoulder, longing to draw her into an embrace again. But he sensed a holy moment and decided to let her talk.

"I met Brian while I was in college. He was a street artist. I asked him why he wasn't an art major, and he said school wasn't for him. That should have been my first clue. He had no problem holding odd jobs and living hand to mouth. But we just clicked, you know? We saw each other off and on for a few years despite my parents' objections. I admit, his looks drew me in. He was a beautiful man. . .on the outside. I never saw the inside until after we were married. He was very talented but had no ambition. We hit the craft-show circuit shortly after our wedding day. Tore my mother's heart out. I had romanticized what it would be like on the road, the people we'd meet and the adventures we'd share. Nothing she could say would change my mind. But after a couple of years on the road, I was ready to settle down and start a family."

She frowned at the darkness of the background as if she could see her life playing there. "We eventually made our way to Oregon. I loved it here and insisted we find a more permanent place to live. Up until then we were basically homeless, living in a camping trailer and mooching off other crafters we met along the way. Finally, after four years of marriage, I found a small but cute apartment in Oakley and told Brian that I was through with traveling. I agreed to find a solid job so he could continue to pursue his art, but if he wanted to travel the circuit, he could do it without me."

Skye hated to see her relive the painful memory. Her down-turned mouth told him that it probably went downhill from there for her and Brian.

"He had always been a drinker, but when I challenged him, it only got worse. He spent my paychecks faster than I could pay the bills. We lived like that for about three years, then one day I gathered all the paintings he'd ever done and signed up for the Oakley craft fair. It was there I met Hannie and David. I fell in love with both of them, and before I realized it, I had told them my whole sob story."

Her finger moved to the leaf hands on the weaving. A tiny smile broke through her past like a ray of sunshine. "Hannie and David prayed with me at the fair. Christ entered my heart right then and there. They invited Brian and me to live in the mobile home on their property as long as we worked for them. I took to the animals right away, and Brian became a handyman, although he wasn't very handy with anything but a paintbrush. I thought surely in this beautiful setting he'd find inspiration for his paintings. That this would turn him around. But I was wrong."

The smile dimmed. "After six months, Brian left. I never heard from him again." She looked up at Skye. Her mouth drew into a thin line. "I learned a few months later that he had died in an accident—DUI."

So Skye's hunch had been correct. Abandonment had left an ugly scar on Ruthanne that nearly matched his own. He took his turn to caress the butterfly, longing to touch this part of her life. "And you stayed here."

"Yes. I guess I proved my worth."

An awkward silence passed between them. Skye sensed that Ruthanne had not planned to launch into her life story.

She glanced around the room, as if remembering why they were there. She swept her hand around the room. "Many of the others also tell a story." She spent the next half hour explaining why Hannie added certain elements to her art. A twig with tender leaves signified the sprout of new life. A piece of oak was stability.

One hanging drew Skye in. It was of the mountains in the fall, with red, yellow, and orange dotting the hillside. Three evergreen trees stood in the foreground—one tall and lush, one brown and dry, seemingly stricken with disease, and one in the middle, also healthy but shorter. He knew beyond any doubt that this represented his birth family, the diseased tree obviously his father. The sky above was a vibrant blue with a swirl of clouds in the corner. When he looked closer, he noticed a cross in the clouds. Perhaps his mother had finally dropped the notion that the sky could solve their problems.

Ruthanne broke into his musing. "Do you ever remember Hannie as being artistic?"

"No, unless you could consider braiding a dandelion chain

as artistic. I do remember her singing though. She did that a lot."

"I have a tape of Hannie singing special music at church. It was over ten years ago, but she still has a beautiful voice. Would you like to hear it sometime?"

Hear his mother's voice? Was he ready for that? He hated to hesitate too long at the simple question. "Uh. . .sure."

"Great, I'll get it to you after we're done here."

Great.

❧

That evening after Ruthanne retired to her mobile home, Skye sat on the carpet in the living room, flipping the cassette tape over and over in his hands. At eye-level with the stereo system on the oak entertainment center, the glowing blue lights from the components stared at him as if wondering what he was waiting for.

Good question.

In the couple of weeks that he'd been on the ranch, he'd learned that his mother had become a Christian and that she had a heart for prisoners, orphans, and substance-abuse patients. She opened her business to the community so they could see the animals up close, and she rescued people like Ruthanne and Tom.

He tapped the cassette on his palm. His mother had become a saint, for crying out loud.

Yet he still had questions. Why did she leave him? Had she been in trouble? That wouldn't have surprised him. But then through the years, she got her life together yet never made contact until now. *Why?*

The word continued to echo in his thoughts. He knew he could never accept all he'd learned about her until that question was answered.

He looked over at Ruddy, sitting on his haunches, tongue dangling, soulful brown eyes staring at him.

"What are you looking at?"

Ruddy slurped his large tongue over his own nose.

"Should I play this? Hear the voice of the woman I've hated all these years?"

Ruddy slid his long front legs to the floor and put his head between his paws.

"You're settling in to hear some music, aren't you?" Skye looked at the plastic case in his hands. "Fine." He opened it and dropped the cassette into the little door. With a push, it clicked into place. His finger hovered over the PLAY button for an eternity before he finally pressed it.

A woman's voice drifted from the speakers—an a cappella version of "I Wonder as I Wander." Although more mature than he remembered, her voice swept him back to his childhood. Sweet moments when she'd sung him to sleep. Or times when just the two of them would take walks and she'd hum whatever tune was popular.

A rough memory surfaced. A time when everyone in the commune had gathered together. His father had died a month before, but Skye didn't miss him. His dad never played with him, just criticized him a lot. They were in a small smoke-filled room. One of many in the house they shared. His mother pulled out her guitar and began to sing. Some silly song of which she botched the words. That always happened when she smoked those little cigarettes. He joined in to help her remember the words.

Someone kicked him in the back. One of the men told him to shut up, that he was ruining the song. Skye looked at his mother. She did nothing—just kept on singing.

His back hurt where the man kicked him. His heart hurt because his mother didn't care. He hated her for that. From that moment on, it seemed she started caring less for Skye and more for where her next fix would come from.

The music from the stereo began squawking. "Oh great!"

Skye punched the EJECT button. "I've broken the machine." He pulled out several inches of tape that had wound around one of the heads. He twirled the tiny plastic wheel in the cassette, trying to wind the tape back in but gave up when he saw how damaged it was. "Now I have to tell Ruthanne I ruined her copy." He spoke to Ruddy, whose head had popped up and tilted during the noise. "I'm going to bed."

At the word "bed," Ruddy rose and limped toward the stairs.

Skye muttered to himself as he followed. "I've broken the barn, my dog, and now Ruthanne's tape." His shoulder and ankle ached from the day's chores. Using his crutch, he set the rubber tip on the step, but Ruddy brushed past him, knocking him off his support. He stumbled and fell against his mother's bedroom door. The knob came in contact with his hand as he balanced himself, but he pulled back sharply.

He clenched his jaw. Some doors should remain shut.

ten

They all arrived at City Park by seven o'clock in the morning. Ruthanne smiled as she stood in their usual prime spot, located under a spreading maple tree, near the beautiful Oakley Creek.

Before unloading, Ruthanne gathered her team of men in a prayer circle where they all held hands. Together they gave thanks for the weather. They also prayed for Hannie's ministry, that her art pieces would touch those who needed it. Skye prayed a hearty prayer for the two alpacas, that they would remain calm and enjoy the attention they would receive. She squeezed his hand to let him know how grateful she was for that prayer, and when he squeezed back, she had to force herself to concentrate on his words. His palm, even with the newly formed calluses, felt comforting and safe as his thumb stroked her finger in an intimate gesture. Her other hand gripped Paul's. Just as strong, just as comforting, but evoking no feelings other than the warmth of friendship.

They set up quickly after that, placing Lirit and Shellie, a golden suri with gorgeous Shirley Temple locks, into the portable pen. Walls made of fabric and PVC pipe became the outdoor gallery for the weavings, and Ruthanne decorated with ribbons and straw flowers she had bought in Merrick.

She brought out the cash drawer from her car and set Skye up at a table with a pad of receipts and a credit card machine. She indicated one of the folding chairs they'd brought. "Have a seat. Holler for Paul or me if you need help with the bigger items."

"Yes, Boss Lady."

She rolled her eyes, thoroughly enjoying his mock reverence.

"Paul, I know you usually do the selling, but if you can help me field questions about the alpacas, I'd appreciate it."

Paul nodded but muttered, "He'd better not mess anything up."

"Well, Skye can't answer alpaca questions very well, can he?" Honestly, men and their egos!

"I'll be back after I feed the animals." Tom excused himself and wandered through the trickle of people who had come out early for the fair.

Ruthanne settled herself behind Hannie's spinning wheel, which thankfully survived the ride in Skye's rented SUV. Before long she had Lirit's carded, washed, and dyed fiber twisting through her fingers. This brought several curious onlookers.

Skye's parents dropped by briefly, his mom excited to see the alpacas up close.

During a lull, Ruthanne decided to stand and stretch. She moved near Skye to check the sales receipts and perhaps catch any errors before Paul did. She needn't have worried though. "You're doing a great job at pushing the merchandise." She grinned as she shuffled the thin papers through her fingers.

"The alpaca toys are an easy sell."

"You've managed to sell some of the larger items, too. We're very grateful to have you here in Hannie's absence."

"Then I guess I made the right decision to do my thirty days sooner rather than later." He reached out and caught her wrist, drawing her near.

"A decision that I praise God for every day." Her heart dipped as she realized their time was growing shorter. "But I'm afraid it will be over much too soon."

"I may move back home, but it needn't be over." He gave her wrist a shake. "I'm just getting to know Calamity."

And Calamity loved getting to know the man behind that midnight kiss.

"Ruthanne." Paul's voice shattered the moment. "If you're not too busy, we have a question over here. *Do you mind?*"

Reluctantly Ruthanne snatched her hand away. Perhaps she shouldn't show open affection for Skye in Paul's presence, but that might be the only way to get through to him. As she moved to Paul's side, she felt Skye's gaze following her.

A middle-aged couple stood near the pen. After Paul introduced them, he took on a friendlier tone, but she sensed tension under his words. "They would like to know the difference between a suri and huacaya alpaca."

She shook her head, perplexed. Paul knew this, but she answered anyway. While she explained the crimping of the different fibers, Paul stood unusually close to her, even for him. As the visitors continued to ask questions, his arm encircled her waist. She once thought of this as one of his touchy-feely actions with no real meaning. But today it had tons of meaning.

Once the man and woman left, Ruthanne extricated herself from his grasp and looked at him. "What was that all about? You didn't need me."

He glanced toward Skye, who was ringing up a small weaving. Paul jammed his hands into his pockets. "Just a little off with our roles switched."

Ruthanne returned to her spinning but couldn't ignore the green-eyed monster that had suddenly inhabited Paul. She should talk with him, explain her feelings for Skye honestly. How many more words would it take to get him to understand? Her frustration translated to the foot pump, and the next ball of fiber thinned in record time.

After a few minutes of therapeutic spinning, familiar squeals came from across the lawn.

"Oh no," Skye mumbled. "The Ya-Ya's have multiplied." He stood as Hannie's entire craft group, consisting of the four from church plus two others, surrounded the area and took him captive. He darted glances about the small booth, apparently looking for an escape route.

"See, doesn't he look like Hannie?" Agnes spoke to the two who hadn't yet met Skye.

Saffron, an ADHD sufferer long before it was invented, allowed her attention to drift before the introductions. "Oh look, they brought the alpacas." She floated away from the pack, her green kerchief blouse billowing like a sail. Agnes, Lark, and Daisy followed Saffron after their brief greetings to Skye, Ruthanne, and Paul.

"Skye, this is Quail and Emerald Dawn," Ruthanne said.

As she made the introductions, he used the table as a buffer between them, as if the women carried germs and he feared infection.

Oh, Skye. Why can't you open up to learn more about Hannie?

Skye harrumphed under his breath. *Ancient hippies.* Lark, Daisy, Saffron, Quail, Emerald Dawn. They had probably forgotten their real names ages ago, except for Agnes, who could have benefited from a flowery name.

Emerald Dawn flipped her long silver-dusted braid over her shoulder. "How's Hannie?"

Ruthanne fielded this question. "I'm. . .confident she'll come out of this as feisty as ever." She stumbled slightly over the word "confident." Was she trying to convince herself as much as the two remaining women?

Quail, who had sold out and used chemicals to dye her hair plum, turned to Skye. "We've wanted to meet you for some time. Hannie is very proud of you."

Emerald Dawn nudged her. A frown creased her already-leathered forehead, and she shook her head.

Confusion swirled around Skye. "How long have you two known about me?"

"Oh, a few years," Quail stammered.

"And my mother has known where I've been all this time?"

Emerald Dawn broke in. "We've known Hannie since her BC days. Before Christ. She was quite despondent in those early years and confessed that she'd had a son, but he was with another family. That wasn't so unusual in our circle of friends.

"But to answer your question: Yes, your mother has known about you. You won a football award in high school. She saw it in the paper. If it hadn't been a color picture, she might not have noticed. But your eyes, and then your name, convinced her that you were her child."

"Well then"—Skye pressed his fists into the table—"maybe you can tell me why she didn't contact me sooner." Anger clawed up his spine.

Ruthanne placed her hand on his arm. "Skye."

He shrugged her off. "No, really. I need to understand this. If she knew where I lived all this time—" He pounded the table and glared at the two hippies, who stood hugging each other.

Skye continued to glower at them, not giving relief. Finally Emerald Dawn let go of her friend and faced him. "I'm sorry, Skye. We don't know. Maybe it was too painful."

He moved around the table and confronted them. "Painful? When she could have done something about it? No, the real pain is knowing your mother doesn't want you anymore, the lost hope that she'll show up and take you home, waking up every morning and wondering what you did wrong. Pain is when the one person you love. . .leaves you."

Turning away from the earth mothers, he spotted Tom talking to a neighboring vendor. Jumping at the opportunity to distance himself, he grabbed his keys from his pocket and threw them onto the table. They landed with a sharp clatter. Ruthanne hugged her arms and gazed at him with tears in her eyes, but he was too angry to care.

"Tom can take over for me. I'm going for a walk. If I'm not

back when you leave, feel free to load my car." Grinding his teeth, he stormed past Paul.

The park had grown thick with fair visitors, and maneuvering through the crowds soon frustrated him. Artsy, nouveau hippies in their fruit-dyed clothes and hemp belts only reminded him of the commune. He walked past a booth selling incense and nearly gagged. That stuff never covered the sickeningly sweet smell of marijuana. Not when twenty people were smoking it.

Memories battered his brain, accompanied by the sitar sound track of a Ravi Shankar tune. Times when his mother was too stoned to realize he hadn't eaten that day. Times when her friends treated him more like a stray dog than a child. Times when all he wanted was a good-night kiss, but Mommy was too busy in another room kissing somebody else.

But Skye had learned so much about his mother in the past few weeks. Why did he allow these voices to take over his good sense? She had obviously changed, so he should embrace that fact and move on. But the emotional scars ran too deep.

He finally found a secluded spot along the river where he could sit and think. He sank to a flat boulder and wrapped his good arm over his head, but it was no use. He couldn't shut out the noise when it came from within.

The happy bubbling of the narrow river flowing at his feet only mocked him. A scattered pile of rocks became his arsenal as he lobbed one after another into the water. Some skipped several times upstream, and others, bombs, aimed at Skye's wandering thoughts as they skittered around like dragonflies. He sat for a long time wallowing in self-pity, but he didn't care. He deserved this moment.

All that time his mother had known where he was. He rocked as his heart broke all over again. *Why?* The question screamed so loud he feared his head would split. Finally he uttered a selfish prayer that she'd recover just so he could ask her that one question.

Somehow opening communication with God helped, and he began to pray with a better attitude. With his knees drawn to his chin and his head bowed, he whispered, "Lord, I'm so tired of feeling this way. How can I accept that my mother has changed? Did she have a good reason for staying away from me? Please, I need to know what she's been thinking all these years."

The strain of a street violin drifted into his small sanctuary. A glance at his watch told him the fair would be winding down soon. Time to go back and help pack up.

ॐ

Ruthanne looked at her watch for the tenth time. Would Skye return before they had to leave?

His outburst had caused feelings that she thought she had conquered. Brian had a temper, and even though he never resorted to physical violence, he often frightened her. Skye had already proved that he was nothing like Brian. Still, she hadn't considered praying for him until twenty minutes ago.

She finally decided she ought to go look for him.

"No, Ruthie. Let him sort this out himself." Paul wrapped his fingers around her elbow, gentle yet sending a message. Had wings of jealousy sent that message? She hoped not.

"I agree, Ruthanne." Tom had already taken the alpacas to the trailer and was dismantling the paddock. "Sometimes a man just needs to be alone."

She glared at them. "A woman would have called five of her best friends by now." When the men turned vacant gazes toward her, she knew she'd lost them with her feminine logic.

Exasperated with the male mind, Ruthanne handed Paul the SUV keys. "Would you please take the spinning wheel to Skye's car? I'll start removing the exhibition pieces and load them in the box."

He wrapped his hand around the keys. "Sure. We did okay today, didn't we?"

"More than okay." The nearly empty booth was a testament to the fact. "Hannie would be proud." She searched the path where Skye had disappeared.

"Why, Paul?" She turned back to Paul, not able to contain her searing question. "Why would Hannie put Skye up for adoption and then not contact him when she settled down?"

"A lot of people do that, Ruthie. Children are adopted out but are seldom contacted by their birth parents."

"But this is Hannie we're talking about. She got her life back on track, married David, and started a business. Why didn't she include her son?"

"She must have her reasons. Do you trust her?"

"Of course I do." But did she?

He thumbed a stray hair from her brow. "Then I'm sure all will come to light."

Ruthanne felt her lip quiver. "If she lives."

Paul shook her shoulders. "Hey, where's that faith you've been preaching?"

She didn't know, but the more she learned about Skye, the more she questioned Hannie.

Paul lifted the spinning wheel, leaving her to her thoughts. This was the second time Skye had run out on her. Thankfully she had his keys so he couldn't trash her barn again. She pulled the tablecloth off and folded it while puzzling through her problem. Yes, he's hurting. But was running a habit of his? Once again she concluded: He wasn't like her husband.

"Am I too late?"

Ruthanne jumped at Skye's voice behind her. "No, we just started tearing down." She wanted to thrust herself into his good arm, but he walked past her and surveyed the work in progress.

Ruthanne sidled next to him. "Are you all right?"

He turned his face to her, a pained expression answering the question. "I will be. Now what do you want me to do?"

Skye seemed to have pulled himself together, but Ruthanne worried about him anyway. He had been hurt deeply, and it pained her that the one person she loved more than life itself had been the cause.

eleven

On Monday morning Ruthanne sipped green tea and stood at the office window watching Skye water the animals. Paul was going over receipts from the craft fair at the desk.

"Skye did pretty well." Ruthanne's respect swelled for the man she had first thought of as an interloper.

"Yeah, before he freaked out on us." Paul placed the receipts in a metal file box and closed the lid. "He really pushed the toys. Now we can deposit a hefty profit into the ministry fund. I've got to admit, I'm surprised at how enthusiastically he's jumped into his role here."

"I think his accident played a big role in that." A giggle bubbled up Ruthanne's throat. "It must be a God thing."

Paul looked at her like she'd lost her mind.

She went on. "Think about it. Before that he was just going through the motions. After the accident he must have felt so much remorse that he dug in and started taking what we do here seriously." She looked back out the window at Skye favoring his arm. "Since his injury is still tender and he can't lift anything heavy for a while, I think we should have him learn what you do."

When she looked back at Paul, his brow had creased into a frown and his shoulders slumped as he leaned his chin into his hand. He looked like someone had stolen his prized spinach tortellini recipe.

"What's wrong?"

Paul glanced up at her. "So he's replacing my job, too?"

"*Too?*"

What new words could she come up with to remind him

they'd never be a couple?

"I'm merely suggesting he learn this side of the business. No one is replacing anybody." She stood behind him and placed her hand on his shoulder. He pulled away with a jerk and stood. "I'm going to see Aunt Hannie. I'll be back tomorrow." Rubbing his neck, he walked out.

The phone shrilled, causing her to jump. The caller ID showed that it was from a friend at animal control.

Although still in shock from Paul's hasty departure, she answered. "Hi, Fred."

After some small talk and an update on Hannie, Fred got to the point of his call. "We confiscated an abused alpaca a few days ago, and the vet has cleared him to leave. I was wondering if you had room for one more."

Ruthanne didn't hesitate. "Of course. Have the owners been charged?"

"You betcha. For neglect. There were several animals on the property—dogs, cats, chickens—all malnourished. We've found homes for the ones that survived, all but the alpaca."

Her heart cried. "I'll come get him today."

"Thanks."

She hung up, seething with righteous indignation. Anyone who neglected another living thing should be hung.

Even if it's Hannie?

She squeezed her eyes shut. No, her biggest supporter could not have neglected Skye. Yet the more she learned about him, the more she could see the possibility. She thought back to the orphanages they had visited together. Those always seemed hardest for Hannie. She'd leave in tears and be useless the rest of the day. It was all beginning to make sense.

Later that afternoon, Ruthanne invited Skye to go along to pick up the alpaca. They followed Fred through the white-tiled corridor where several different kinds of animals rested in wire cages. Out the back door, where the larger animals convalesced, the tiny huacaya alpaca stood in a corner of a small-penned area. His grunts of distress tore at Ruthanne's heart.

When she saw the little guy, barely five months old and a mere skeleton under matted light rose gray fiber, her anger burned anew. "I hope they throw the book at them," she muttered as Skye knelt in front of him. He stroked the alpaca's neck, and Ruthanne marveled at the bond forming right before her eyes.

He crooned soft words. "It's okay—you're safe now. No one can hurt you any longer."

A shiver crept through Ruthanne as she realized someone may have said those very words to Skye once.

Ruthanne carried the cria to the car. Skye slipped into the passenger seat and held out his good arm. Pride warmed her heart as she watched this ever-changing man snuggle the alpaca in his lap. The cria immediately laid his head on Skye's shoulder. "He already trusts you."

"Yeah, well, we're cut from the same cloth."

Ruthanne prayed silently for this man who had apparently known neglect. She also prayed for herself, that her view of Hannie wouldn't be colored by what might eventually be revealed.

❧

The tiny alpaca shivered in Skye's arms for the first few miles then relaxed. Skye thought of his heavenly Father. How He had held him through the rough times. He couldn't feel God's arms at first, but as Skye's faith and trust grew, so did his sense of security.

When they arrived home, Tom's truck sat in the driveway, loaded down with lumber for the barn. They had been fixing the damage slowly the past week, tearing out the splintered boards and hauling off debris, and were now poised to rebuild the wall. Tom, however, must have been off doing other chores while he waited on Skye.

Ruthanne threw the gearshift into PARK then walked around to help Skye with the cria. He reluctantly released him into her care.

The alpaca twisted and groaned in Ruthanne's arms as Skye slid out of the car. She tried soothing words, but there was no response. "Okay! My, what a fuss." When Skye was on his feet again, she gave the alpaca back, placing it in his good arm and helping him balance with the injured one against the shoulder sling.

The alpaca settled down immediately, prompting Skye's protective instincts. "I'll carry him in from here. He can't weigh more than twenty-five pounds."

"Half the weight he should be. But he'll grow under your care." She grinned at him. "Looks like you're Papa now."

They entered the cria's new stall where Skye set him down. When Ruthanne handed him a prepared bottle, he felt grateful that he could do more.

"Hold the bottle here"—she indicated a few feet off the ground—"to simulate the mother's undercarriage." Skye delighted in seeing the cria, tentative at first, eventually attack the bottle. He laughed as new feelings of protection and provision surged through him. "I guess I'm Mama, too."

"I guess you are." Ruthanne laughed.

When the bottle was empty, Skye lowered himself to the floor and leaned against the wall. The cria curled up into a small ball, snuggled against Skye, and fell asleep.

Ruthanne stood near them. "After he's rested and gotten used to his surroundings, I'll introduce him to Hershey. She's a wonderful mom, so maybe she'll adopt him."

Skye buried his fingers in the soft alpaca wool, wanting to continue to offer comfort even though the animal slept. Ruthanne knelt in front of him, her green eyes crinkling in approval. Skye grinned back at her. It felt great to do something right for a change.

"So," she said while gently stroking the alpaca's thin neck. "What are you going to name him?"

"Me?"

"Of course. He's yours now."

He's mine. Skye remembered the first time he owned a pet. Skye's adoption was final, and the puppy was his gift to welcome him to the family. He'd owned other animals afterward, but this one had remained special because it meant a family had accepted him. It was their way of saying, *You aren't going anywhere, buddy, and we're going to make your stay here permanent.*

That's how he felt with this alpaca. Like Lirit for Ruthanne, this new charge would make his stay, or at least his ties to the ranch, permanent. He decided to give him the same name he gave the puppy.

"Destry."

Ruthanne cocked an eyebrow. "Interesting name."

He laughed at her perplexed expression. "Destry was a character that Audie Murphy played in an old Western. He was this small cowboy who did big things."

She nodded her approval. "And with your guidance, I'm sure the same is in store for our little Destry."

"Our little Destry." He liked the sound of that.

Ruthanne left. About a half hour later, Skye heard hammering. He began to feel guilty for sitting around while Tom worked on the barn, so he quietly extricated himself from Destry's side.

The two men worked on the wall for a couple of hours before it started to get dark. Despite the long ponytail, a reminder that this man was an ex-hippie, he liked Tom. They seemed to be in harmony on many different levels.

Especially their love of the Lord.

They got to talking about their conversions while Tom inspected a board for straightness.

Tom started. "Hannie and David found me at the prison."

"Were you a guard?"

"Nope. An inmate."

Skye's brows shot up. "Really?"

Tom set the board's end on the ground and leaned on it like a staff. "In those days, I stole from convenience stores for drug money."

Skye swallowed hard. Did it have to be for drugs?

"I connected with David, and he promised to give me a job if I cleaned myself up. The day before, I had been contemplating where I could meet my supplier when I got out." He placed the board on two sawhorses.

"What was it that David said that made you turn your life around?" Skye breathed in the fresh pine smell from the wood and steadied the board while Tom sawed through it, still awed that someone so similar to his mother had changed his life so drastically.

Tom stopped sawing. "It wasn't so much his words. I'd heard it all before and rejected it. But the alpaca they brought. . . When that animal looked at me with such trust as I fed it a peanut, I realized there was so much more to life than getting high." He pushed the saw through the board once more and stopped. "And I asked myself, 'How many other wonders are out there that I'm too fuzzy to see?' I knelt right there in the rec room and accepted Jesus as my Savior. And when I got out, David gave me that job and an ultimatum to stay clean or he'd boot me out."

"What a great testimony."

"Oh, I'm not saying it was easy. But without God, I'd never have been able to break free." He swept away the sawdust and walked to where he would nail up the board. "What about you, son? How long have you known the Lord?"

Skye never felt easy talking about his past. But something about this man drew it out of him. "I lived with my birth parents in a commune when I was little. My dad died, and my mother. . ." He wanted to say his mother couldn't wait to get rid of him, but this was Hannie. Tom had idolized her along with everyone else in her world. He decided to leave that part out. "I ended up in the foster system. Shuffled around like an unwanted gift. Then a Christian couple adopted me. They led me to the Lord with their love and patience."

Tom searched through the nail box with a meaty finger. "Not an easy task, I assume."

Skye chuckled. "You could say that."

The last board went up, and Tom declared the job finished except for the paint.

Skye wasn't ready to end the fellowship though. He clasped Tom's shoulder. "I just brought home a new addition to my family. Would you like to see him?"

Tom nodded and followed Skye to the barn.

When they walked into the stall, Tom grinned. "Well, look at that."

Destry had found a new playmate, a black suri that stood only a half head taller.

Ruthanne stood in the corner, a smug look on her face. "I told you Hershey would make a great mom. And now Destry has a brother."

"Destry?" Tom's shocked expression surprised Skye.

"Yes, after my favorite cowboy."

Tom knelt to pat the alpaca on his neck. "Audie Murphy."

"You like old Westerns?"

Tom cleared his throat and rubbed his nose. "Sure do. Maybe we'll rent one sometime."

They watched the two adoptive brothers romp, affording Skye an opportunity to ponder this strange man. Going to prison for drugs? Still, he had turned his life around and become a Christian.

But isn't that what Skye's mother did? Why could he

accept that a stranger could reform but his mother could not?

He ground his teeth. Because it wasn't just the drugs. There was the other little question that needed answering. What he wanted to ask her that first day in the hospital. *Why? Why did you leave me?*

twelve

"Remind me why we're doing this?" Skye tackled the unpleasant job. How had he gotten roped into this one?

"Alpacas need to be sheared," Ruthanne answered like a patient teacher. "That's how we get the fiber for the products like those we sold at the craft fair a week ago."

"No, the other thing." Sweat tickled his temple, and he wiped it away with his sleeve.

Ruthanne sighed. "Singing Mountain Ranch hosts Shearing Day for all the area ranchers because we have the most acreage to work in. We all contribute money to hire professional shearers so it gets done faster."

"That's not what I mean."

"Oh. You mean, why are we stuffing mushrooms?"

"Yeah." Skye crinkled his nose. This was definitely not his forte. At first he thought the worst thing was cleaning the slippery bulbs. But even his hen-pecked egg gathering was preferable to holding the caps still while he shoved a mixture of cream cheese and chopped vegetables into them. "Why can't we serve hot dogs and hamburgers like every other American?"

"We are, but Paul has to show off. I think he's outdone himself this time though. There's enough food here to feed not only the workers but the animals, too."

"How can he afford this?" Another mushroom cap slipped from his fingers, and a glob of cream cheese landed in his palm. "Where is he anyway?" Skye glanced around the kitchen while rinsing his hand in the sink. "At home putting the finishing touches on the fatted calf?"

"Relax. He'll be right back. He got an important phone call and needed to meet some people. He's on the verge of starting his own catering business. At affairs like ours, he asks for donations, and if the money is short, he writes that off as advertising. His goal is to get his food in front of people so they'll ask him to their next event."

"Oh, so we're the guinea pigs."

"Exactly."

Their easy banter warmed Skye. Despite the unpalatable task of the day—he hated fungi—he enjoyed being with Ruthanne and hearing her laughter.

She wiped her hands on a towel and slid the cookie sheet of filled mushrooms into the refrigerator. "Once we're done with the food, can you help me sort out the vaccinations? I give the animals their shots on Shearing Day since the alpacas are already contained. It helps to have all the syringes prepared per their weight and tagged with their names so I don't have to worry about getting the right dosages at the last moment."

"Smart." Skye nodded.

He had been working on the ranch for almost four weeks and learned something new every day. Tomorrow would be the much-anticipated Shearing Day, and he looked forward to seeing the process. Even though his shoulder still ached, he was determined to pull his weight.

Around eight o'clock the next morning, two men, one younger and one older, arrived with their shearing equipment. Skye showed them where to set up in the barn.

"Is this a family business?" Skye asked while they laid out their shearing supplies, the long-toothed razors resembling torture devices more than barbering tools.

"Dad here started it after being raised on a sheep ranch." The younger, thirtyish man referred to his older counterpart.

"Yep," the older man answered. They both had sandy

brown hair, but the senior's had faded, with infiltrating strands of gray. "I found out I liked shearin' 'em more than watchin' 'em."

"Dad's the master shearer in the area, and anyone who needs to get a coat off an animal calls him."

Activity outside the barn door caught Skye's attention. The area ranchers were arriving. "By the looks of that crowd out there, you must be doing pretty well."

"Not bad. We serve all of Oregon and northern California. Hey, could you grab one of those tarps there and spread it out? The fleece falls on it as we shear so it's easier to drag away and bag." The father-son team excused themselves to retrieve more supplies from their trailer.

After struggling to open the tarp with one arm, he removed the sling and gingerly tested it for movement. The numbness was gone. Maybe if he was careful and only used his left arm to help steady the larger stuff—

"What do you think you're doing, mister?" Ruthanne rushed to his side.

"I'm fine." He gently slapped her hands away from the sling that now dangled from his neck.

"You're not fine. The doctor said you'd need to keep this on for a full month."

He captured her wrist as she tried to stuff his arm back into the sling. "Ruthanne."

She turned a worried gaze up to him while leaning into his arm to keep it from lowering.

"I'll be careful."

"But—"

"I'm going to do this. If I feel pain, I'll put it back on."

"Promise?"

He released her wrist and held up two fingers for the pact. "Alpaca Apprentice honor."

She grinned then seemed to notice her other arm was

hugging his body. When she started to move away, he caught her and pulled her tighter.

"I do like you worrying about me though." He kissed her forehead. "Makes me feel all tingly."

"That's your injury, silly."

"No it's not." He kissed her nose.

"Are you going to stand there and argue—"

He kissed her mouth. The protective arms that had surrounded him now slipped up to his neck.

"Um. . .excuse us." The two shearers stood behind Ruthanne with laughter in their eyes.

"Oh! Sorry." Ruthanne blushed as she broke away to help, leaving Skye wanting more of her kisses but also leaving him annoyed that she could so easily grab the heavy object they struggled with while he could not.

"What is that?" Skye watched as they set up a large six-foot by four-foot board attached to a swivel mechanism and legs. He had compared the various clippers to torture devices, but this thing looked absolutely gruesome.

"The tipping table." Ruthanne pressed her hip against the vertical board. "The alpaca is placed here." Then the two men flipped a bar in the back, tilting the table and lifting Ruthanne so she now lay on top. From her side, she waved in the air. "And voilà! Minimal stress to the animal, and it saves the shearers' backs."

"Cool." Skye looked forward to seeing it used.

The neighboring ranchers trickled in during the next hour, parking their trailers around back. Tom and Skye helped the visitors move their animals into empty stalls. This seemed a good day for the ranchers to check out the other herds. On a couple of occasions throughout the morning, Skye overheard conversations as people bartered their herd sires—a strapping male for another's flawless female. Any offspring of Gabriel's were looked at carefully, and approving nods seemed to please Ruthanne, who bustled around making sure everyone felt welcome and knew what they were doing.

By midmorning, portable corral panels set up an aisle leading into the barn. Several teams formed quickly and began their duties on the assembly line.

Ruthanne gave Skye his instructions. "Follow each animal through the process so you can get a feel of how it's done. I don't mind you stopping to help, but if I see you with so much as a nail clipper in your left hand, I'll send you to the pasture to harvest beans. Got it?" The hand on her hip negated the smile on her lips. Skye had no doubt she'd follow through on her threat.

"Yes, Boss Lady!" He snapped a smart salute and did an about-face, marching off to his designated station.

A visiting white and black dappled huacaya named Oreo was the first customer. She minced her way, clearly uncertain of her handler's intentions as he led her to the first station. Skye stood alongside the team that picked larger pieces of debris off the coats. He reached in and grabbed leaves, chunks of dirt, and pieces of hay off the fuzzy coat. Another customer waited, so he and the two other volunteers picked up the pace.

He followed Oreo down the aisle to the next station. The roar of two Shop-Vacs didn't help Oreo's nervous condition, but the women wielding them did so with deft movements as they vacuumed any remaining rubbish out of the fleece.

"Why not just rinse them off?" Skye raised his voice, competing against the noise. When he got his haircut, the barber always did it wet.

"Because their coats would be too heavy for the shearers," one of the women answered. "Some people still do it that way, but then the animal has to either be blown dry or sent back out to pasture to dry off. If they roll out there, the whole procedure has to be done all over again. We've found this method cuts down the preparation significantly."

By now the assembly line had filled. Two alpacas were in the grooming aisle, and a third now waited its turn. Skye rushed into the barn and joined Ruthanne just in time to see Oreo tipped into her lying position. She seemed only minimally distressed, groaning softly.

"See?" Ruthanne pointed to the table. "It would be so much harder to force her to lie down on the ground. She would get upset and wouldn't lie still."

Skye laughed as the two men quickly finished one side and flipped the alpaca to her other side before she knew what they were doing. "So I guess *torture* is not the word of the day."

"No." She giggled with him. "The real torture comes the next day when you try to get out of bed."

The plastic tarp he had laid out earlier caught the thick blanket of wool from Oreo's back and sides. Some teenage boys and girls pulled the tarp away while others replaced it. The shearers then shaved the neck and upper legs of the animal.

"They're shearing the seconds now," Ruthanne said. "That is less desirable hair, shorter and coarser. After the skirting process, it can be used in batting for quilts or for hand spinning. It won't be as soft as the first cut."

"I had no idea it was such a science."

"Oh, I haven't even touched on DNA matches and special breeding to obtain the choicest fiber."

Skye put his hands over his ears. "Stop. I'm on overload already."

"And just wait until we get into the dyes."

"Hey, what's this over here?" He put a stop to the lecture by tugging her to another station in the spacious barn.

Six women sat around a four-foot by six-foot framed metal screen, balancing it on their knees.

"This is the skirting table. They already have the first batch of fleece on there, cut side down."

The women pulled at the fleece blanket to loosen the fibers then vigorously shook the screen. Underneath, a shower of debris particles and hair fell out of the bottom. Strong, experienced hands searched through the fleece, pinching and pulling.

"What are they finding in there? Wasn't the vacuuming enough?"

"There are always burrs, stubborn bits of hay, and grain stuck in the fiber deep down."

As they found the debris, they tossed it to the floor. When they were finished, more volunteers stuffed the fleece into a clear plastic bag.

"They will tag the bags with the owner's name, and these kids here"—she indicated some older children waiting on the floor—"will drag them to a corner of the barn. When the animals are finished, the ranchers can pick up their bags and go home."

"So." Skye glanced around at the clockworklike activity. "Every person who brings their animals pitches in." He liked that kind of teamwork. It spoke to his sense of organization.

The volunteers on floor patrol swept away a large chunk of hair and tossed it into the trash. "Whatever happened to 'nothing wasted'?"

Ruthanne wrinkled her nose. "This is hair that can't be salvaged. It's not only very coarse but the litter inside is impossible to get out. It's just easier to toss it."

When Oreo was done, they released her down another aisle, where she bounded out to pasture.

Ruthanne left him for a little while to do her part on the assembly line. He continued to ask questions and help haul bags, and he even took a turn at the skirting table.

An hour later Ruthanne grabbed his arm. "Come on. This is the best part of the whole day."

His stomach growled, and he looked at his watch. "Lunch?"

Where had the morning gone?

"No, something better."

They headed out to the pasture where the sheared alpacas frolicked after their release. Several skinny, alien-looking creatures rolled in the dust, their long skeletal necks writhing in pure joy. He laughed at the ones standing to the side, looking indignant at the atrocities they had just endured. With their body coats gone, their heads looked huge, as if the spindly necks would never be able to hold them up.

Some of the teenagers had the fun job of sprinkling down the newly shorn with a hose.

"They don't look too traumatized." He laughed along with the crowd who had gathered to watch. It seemed many of the workers decided to take their breaks at that moment. The alpacas romped in the droplets, relishing the feel of the water on their skin.

"I think the end more than justifies the means." Ruthanne dodged a stream of water that flew off the head of a dancing alpaca.

"It must feel good to get all that fur off their bodies." He felt the warmth of the day seeping through his shirt. "Especially as we go into the summer months."

"There are days in the winter when I wish I had their thick coats, but I can't imagine keeping it all year long. Some ranchers prefer not to shear the pregnant animals. But since we hire professionals, we go ahead."

His stomach growled again, and this time it did not go unnoticed.

Ruthanne laughed as she looked at her watch. "It's time."

"Really? We can eat?"

"Let me check with Paul in the kitchen, but I'm sure he'll be prompt."

Together they made the break announcement, which made them very popular.

Before eating, Ruthanne called all those gathered for the blessing. As she prayed, Skye raised his face to the warm sun—neither too hot nor too cold, with cotton clouds filtering the sun's rays.

Thank You, Lord, for this beautiful day, for Ruthanne and her patience, and yes. . .even for the circumstances that have led me here. I trust You to finish what You've started. Remembering his unsettled business with his mother, he offered a disclaimer. *I know I say all this while I'm happy. Please remind me of this prayer if things don't go my way. Amen.*

He shook off the foreboding feeling that God had something more for him to learn, something that had nothing to do with alpaca shearing, something that he didn't want to face.

Paul had set up tables under the back deck in the shade. A wicker basket perched on a corner to gather money for the food. Hungry volunteers swarmed as if the doors had just opened on a Harry & David's buy-one-get-one-free sale. Some took their food up to the deck, and others sat under the trees scattered around the property.

Along with a hot dog and hamburger, Skye filled his plate with food he couldn't identify. Had he heard the word *canapé* at the table? He tasted salmon, cream cheese, and dill. And what were those odd little lettuce wraps filled with spicy ground beef, coleslaw, and green onions? He deliberately avoided the stuffed mushrooms. Even if he liked fungi, too many of those puppies had ended up on the floor when he was cleaning them. He settled under a maple tree in the north pasture, his arm a little sore from the day's activities. Several teenage girls invaded his spot. They chattered like the birds in the maple tree outside his bedroom window, reminding him of his youngest sister, Robyn.

Ruthanne eventually joined them. "Whenever you girls are done, Francie could use your help in the barn."

They all jumped up at once, and the giggling gaggle of girls disappeared back into the barn.

"Sorry about that. You probably didn't need all that energy when you were trying to rest."

"That's okay. They entertained me." He chuckled while scrutinizing a lettuce thing.

"Not a gourmet connoisseur?" Her eyes, green as the pasture grass, crinkled as she smiled.

"Um. . .think I'll get another hot dog."

He glanced toward the house where Paul moved about with trays of food to replenish his emptying table. But when he returned the look, Skye suddenly felt uncomfortable. He still wasn't clear on a few things.

"Other than his strange sense of picnic fare, Paul seems to be a great guy."

Her eyes sparkled—not what Skye wanted. "Oh, he's been my best friend ever since I moved to the ranch." *"Friend."* Noted. "No one could ask for a better pal." *"Pal." Even better.* "When Brian left, Paul helped pick up the pieces. He became my rock." *"Rock." That's a step in the wrong direction.*

He had shared only two kisses with Ruthanne, the first that night of the screaming alpaca scare. Had the moon been to blame for their slip into romanticism? Probably. That and the fact that Ruthanne was intoxicated with victory. That poor paint-splattered mutt never stood a chance. He chuckled at the memory.

"What?" She frowned at him.

"What do you mean, 'What'?" He feigned innocence.

"You're laughing. Let me in on the joke."

"I was just thinking of the other night when you graffitied the neighbor's dog."

She blushed crimson as if she'd been the one shot with a paint gun. He guessed she was thinking of the moon as well. Or perhaps their latest kiss just hours earlier in the barn.

"Oh, I never told you. It worked. I called them the next day to see if they noticed."

"And?"

"Of course they did. A black dog with neon yellow splotches? I confessed, offered to pay the groomer to get him clean, and told them if I saw him over here again, I'd use buckshot."

"That's my Calamity."

He decided to plunge into the real reason he started this conversation. "So, back to Paul. Just how good of a *friend* is he?" His gaze held hers so there could be no doubt as to why he asked that question.

She swallowed.

"Ruthie!" Paul called from the deck. "Where are the small paper plates you said you had?"

"I'll be right there!" She turned to Skye. "I'm sorry, I have to help him." She sprang up and ran to the house.

Had she deliberately ignored his question?

For the rest of the afternoon, Skye and Ruthanne were never together long enough for even a short, intimate conversation. His question continued to hang in the air like a neighbor's unreturned wave.

Yet she continued to glance at him with—dare he think?—flirtatious looks that made him wish the day would go faster so he could kiss her again.

During an afternoon break, Paul laid out several desserts provided by the visiting ranchers. The little paper plates sat in stacks. Had he really needed help finding them?

Skye ended up near the barn in an exchange of funny alpaca stories with several ranchers. But he could see the back of the house where he had a ringside seat to the Paul and Ruthanne Show. They stood behind the dessert table, acting as host and hostess. Paul would say something funny—Ruthanne would laugh. He'd bump her shoulder playfully—she'd slap his. It all looked very much like a brother-and-sister act. At least on her part. But he feared that Paul was more serious. Skye had never been particularly intuitive, but the man's eyes kept darting in his direction.

That pained Skye in a small way. He scratched his chin. How was he going to date Ruthanne without hurting Paul?

❧

Every year during Shearing Day, Ruthanne felt in her element as she cohosted with Hannie. But this year, besides the fact that Hannie wasn't there, things had changed. And that change stood a few yards away by the paddocks, watching her with those clear blue eyes.

She'd thought of their first kiss often. And today her heart hadn't stopped humming since he kissed her in the barn.

However, her practical self warred within her. She'd been a widow only three years. Was she ready for a boyfriend?

Another thing to consider was Hannie, who had so wanted to see Ruthanne and her nephew together. The poor dear had played Cupid so many times that Ruthanne feared she'd run out of arrows.

But wouldn't Hannie be just as pleased if Ruthanne got together with her son?

And *there* was the elephant in the room.

Hannie and Skye had no mother-son relationship. Skye clearly held animosity toward his mother. In light of that, how could Ruthanne and Skye have a healthy intimacy?

So many questions, which was why she couldn't answer him right away. She tossed up a quick prayer for guidance and tagged on a small request.

If Skye isn't for me, would You please silence this silly humming?

thirteen

As a tradition, one of the area ranchers always thought of fun things to do to wind down from Shearing Day. This year for the group, he booked a cruise with Rogue River Hellgate Jetboat Excursions for the next Sunday afternoon.

Skye had heard of the cruise but never had the opportunity to go. It sounded like fun, with high speeds on the water and a meal downriver.

The morning of the cruise Skye once again visited Ruthanne's church and found it only mildly annoying when people talked about his mother. Perhaps he was becoming numb to all the Hannie praise.

Afterward Skye found Ruthanne and Paul in the foyer, deep in discussion.

"I wish you'd reconsider, Paul." She looked at him with concern in her eyes.

"Reconsider what?" Skye nudged his way into the conversation.

Paul rubbed the back of his neck. "I'm not going on the cruise."

"Why not? It won't be the same without you."

"Well, I have to work, and—"

"Didn't you tell me you don't work on Sunday mornings?"

"Yes. . .but. . .I've got tons of work to do at the ranch."

"You worked hard enough yesterday." Skye waved away that thought. "Today you should reward yourself."

Ruthanne had been unusually quiet during this exchange, and he placed his hand on her back. "Talk to him." Her warmth radiated to his hand, and Skye suddenly wondered why he was trying to convince Paul to go.

"I've tried talking to him, but he doesn't like the—"

"The fuss," Paul interrupted her. "I don't like all the fuss. Why celebrate something that's your job to begin with?"

"Okay then." Skye shrugged. "We'll miss you."

He started to walk away, and when a frowning Ruthanne followed under his arm, slipping her hand around his waist, he could barely hear Paul for his heart thumping hard in his chest.

"Wait!" Paul joined them. "You're right. I should enjoy myself after working so hard yesterday."

Ruthanne cocked an eyebrow. "Then you're going?"

"Yes." He cast a glance at her arm around Skye. "I think I'd better."

About sixty people who had been involved in the shearing gathered in Grants Pass later that afternoon. The forecast promised a sunny and warm day, but the smart Oregonians brought their Windbreakers, just in case. Skye allowed Ruthanne to pull him down the dock while Paul dragged behind.

"Come on, pokey." Ruthanne grabbed Paul's arm and placed herself between the two men.

The entire group fit into the boat as they sat on the blue benches. Each bench sat six people, and Skye found himself on the end. "I wonder how wet I'll get." He looked over the edge at the dark swirling river water.

Their tour guide, who piloted from a taller platform at the back of the boat, told everyone to hang on. He took off in a swirling pin curl that caused a centrifugal force with the five people on the bench. They all slid like beads on an abacus, squishing Ruthanne into Skye's hip. Yep. He was going to like this excursion.

"Better than an amusement park!" Ruthanne's eyes danced.

Skye placed his arm on the back of her seat and cocked his head as he regarded her. "I didn't know you were a daredevil."

She whispered into his ear. "How do you think I got the name *Calamity*?"

The boat took off and drove his laughter back into his throat. Wind blew past his face, taking with it all his cares.

Ruthanne squealed as if she were on a roller coaster. He delighted in that sound as much as her soft giggles. She cast a concerned glance at Paul, though, who white-knuckled the seat in front of him, his mouth a straight slash across his face—and was that terror in his eyes?

Soon the boat slowed down. After the applause, the guide said, "That was a little taste of what we'll experience later on."

During a more leisurely pace, the guide pointed out some stunning nature: an eagle soaring overhead with a fish grasped in its claws, a deer and her fawn getting a drink, osprey landing amid the white bell-like flowers of a shedding madrone.

Eventually the shore began to close in on them. "We're about to go through the infamous Hellgate Canyon." The tour guide eased back the throttle, and the boat floated toward an ever-narrowing passage that sliced a gash through layers of stone. "If you've ever seen the movie *Rooster Cogburn* with John Wayne, this is where he escaped the bad guys on the river raft."

Skye loved that Western. He joined the rest on board as they nodded, recalling that scene.

As they glided through the canyon, appropriately named Hellgate, Skye tipped his head back. Two craggy walls towered above them, revealing a narrow slit of daylight at the top. He swallowed hard. Nothing like a dose of nature's grandeur to restore a man's humility. In the shadows, he thought about God. His love had eroded the hard places away in his heart. Hard places that could have eventually opened a gate to destruction. Even as a child he had resisted that love, but it slowly carved a path, reshaping him into the adult he eventually became.

The short gorge finally opened as they made their way

through to the other side of the hill, and the pilot sped away, eliciting cheers from the passengers.

Skye cast a glance over at Paul, who had not only seized the chair in front of him but had added extra comfort by wrapping his arm around Ruthanne's right elbow. Skye looked at her fingers to see if they were turning blue. "You okay there, bud?"

"Yeah." Paul's shaky reply suggested anything but. "Just wondering how those rocks stayed glued to the mountainside."

Ruthanne patted his hand. "Have faith."

He seemed to get the message and rode the rest of the way untethered to her.

Finally they reached their destination.

"As you get out of the boat," the guide explained, "the OK Corral is a good stretch of the legs uphill. You can choose to walk the short incline or take the free limo that will be waiting for you."

Skye chuckled when he saw the "limo" was a John Deere tractor pulling a flat, open trailer with seats. Ruthanne wanted the whole experience, so she bounded toward the tractor.

On the ride up the hill, her face lit up as she took in the surroundings. "This place is so beautiful. The river. The evergreen trees. The manicured lawn. Who would have thought an old homestead would have a lawn?" When the large mountain-lodge-looking structure came into view, she could barely contain herself. "That's not a homestead. It's too grand."

Skye loved her enthusiasm. He'd never seen this side of her, and he suspected this was the true Ruthanne, before his mother's illness caused the worry shadows on her face.

The group congregated under a large covered patio held up by honed logs. Wooden handmade chairs pressed against long tables draped with red-checkered tablecloths. Shiny white dishes and clear glasses finished the display. This all lent a homey yet elegant feel to their dining experience.

"When I heard we were eating at an old settlement, I

pictured a backyard barbecue and paper plates." Skye gazed around in awe.

"Rustic yet elegant." Ruthanne nodded in agreement.

Aromas straight from Grandma's kitchen filtered to the outside dining room, and Skye chose their seats quickly, eager to get started. Soon the food arrived family style in bowls and on platters. Everyone passed the delicious barbecued ribs, fried chicken, corn bread, and biscuits, and began visiting in one collective noise. Except Paul. Apparently he was still upset from the boat ride. He picked at his food and criticized every little thing.

"Too much pepper."

"Dressing's too thin."

At one point, Skye feared that Paul might storm the kitchen to teach the chef how to cook.

Ruthanne tried to make up for Paul's rudeness by placating him. "What's in this honey-mustard dressing, Paul? There's a mystery ingredient I can't identify."

Dessert included Apple Brown Betty, which Skye and Ruthanne discovered they both loved.

"I like it, too," Paul interrupted them. He stood and pitched his napkin to the table. "A lot!" Then he stormed away.

Ruthanne turned a shocked gaze at Skye. "What was that all about?"

"I don't know." But he suspected. Paul's performance throughout the day suggested a jealous alter ego lurking behind the mild-mannered chef.

After dessert they were encouraged to stretch their legs and check out the terrain. The boat would be leaving in an hour. Skye had eaten so much he feared he'd waddle. He excused himself to use the facilities, and when he returned, both Ruthanne and Paul had disappeared. He chatted with the other guests for a while, but he worried that Paul might be swaying Ruthanne to choose between them. Either that or she had pulled him aside like a disobedient child to verbally punish him for his behavior.

He chose to believe that last train of thought and patiently waited for them to rejoin the group.

❧

Ruthanne stomped along the gravel path trailing the river. When she finally cooled down enough to talk, she turned and confronted him. "What was all that about during dinner?"

He opened his mouth to speak, but nothing came out. She assumed he was about to give an unconvincing excuse. Finally he shoved his hands into the pockets of his jacket and looked out at the river. "Is it truly only a friendship you want from me?" The quiet question thundered in her ears.

"Paul. . ." She reached out for his arm. "We tried dating. Remember? It didn't work out."

"You said you weren't ready so soon after becoming a widow." His gaze searched her face. "It's been three years, Ruthie."

"I know, but—"

"But you'll never be serious about me."

She pondered a pile of rocks along the path. "No. I don't feel—"

"You don't feel for me the way you do Skye."

She jerked her gaze back to him. "I was going to say I don't feel worthy of your attention. I know you've had feelings for me, and I selfishly allowed them because I needed to feel loved after Brian left. You were safe."

He snorted. "That's not what a guy in love wants to hear."

"Really, Paul? Love? If you loved me, you wouldn't have waited this long to tell me so. In fact, if it weren't for Skye's attention, you might have let this go on for another three years."

He picked at a piney knob on a nearby tree. "Maybe I needed you, too. My love for Aunt Hannie must have spilled over, and I really liked taking care of you both." He grinned.

"Neither of you can cook."

"That's true." She laughed, grateful their little tiff was ending. "We might have starved if it weren't for you."

They stood in silence for a moment. Ruthanne imagined the smoothly flowing river carrying away any misunderstandings between them.

"*Do* you love me, Paul?"

"I don't know." An errant twig springing from the tree suffered abuse as Paul twisted it unmercifully. "I guess you were safe for me, too."

Ruthanne turned from the river to give him her full attention. "How so?"

"When you moved in with my aunt and uncle, remember how we clicked?"

"Of course. I could always talk to you."

Paul, who had decimated the twig, now turned his attention on a small, leafy plant, loosening its roots with his toe. He turned his gaze toward her. "I figured we'd continue on forever."

"Forever is fine for a friendship. But if there is a commitment with no love, forever can drag agonizingly slow. Believe me. I know."

After a moment of silence, Paul spoke softly. "I want you as a friend, Ruthanne."

She allowed his words to shower over her. "Me, too. I don't want to lose you just because I'm interested in someone else." She touched his arm. "But I need to be free to pursue other romantic interests. If Skye isn't the one, there will be others. Can you handle that?"

Paul slouched lazily against the tree, his grin drawing out the Paul she had come to love—or rather, *like* in an intense, brotherly way. "Hey, can *you* handle it if *I* meet someone else?"

"I'll do you one better. I'll start praying for someone who will make your heart sing."

As they started back down a path leading to the boat,

Ruthanne told him about her gauge for knowing God's will.

"I like Skye, believe it or not." Paul picked his way through the light brush, clearing a path for her to walk. "It could have been worse. I could have lost you to Gerald from church."

She wrinkled her nose. "Gerald? That skinny kid who had a crush on me?"

He tossed over his shoulder, "Pimples and all!"

❧

Skye glanced at his watch—again. He'd already wandered down to the boat but was prepared to launch a full manhunt if his two companions failed to show up. With only ten minutes to spare before the boat took off without them, Paul and Ruthanne stepped out of the woods and walked toward him. He'd half expected Paul to be dragging behind like a puppy that had just had its nose smacked. But instead his easy smile remained in place. Ruthanne grabbed his shoulders from behind and said something into his ear, then glanced toward Skye. Paul nodded, waved at him, and boarded the boat.

Skye joined Ruthanne, and they strolled downriver, being careful not to stray too far. Her silence created a lasso that squeezed his gut. Was she about to break up with him before they even began?

She finally stopped and turned to face him. The sun had begun its descent and glittered on the roving current like diamonds on a necklace. "I never answered your question."

He racked his brain to remember what he'd asked. "What question?"

"The other day you asked how good a friend Paul was." Her smile held him hostage as she paused. "The answer is, a very good friend."

His heart sank. She was about to defend her feelings for Paul. But then she said, "And *only* a friend."

Her green eyes sparkled, emeralds rivaling the diamonds in the river. When she took a step toward him, all his questions fell away and clattered to the forest floor. He wrapped his arms around her waist and thoroughly kissed the lips that had just freed him to love her.

☙

Paul hopped into his car when they returned to the ranch. Instead of kissing Ruthanne's temple before she got out of the car, he chucked her chin and called her "pal." Skye guessed that was a result of their talk earlier. Then he waved to Skye as he pulled out.

Skye slipped his hand into Ruthanne's while they strolled toward the paddocks to check on the animals. Her answering gaze created a love rhythm as his heart beat against his chest. Dusk began to deepen into evening, creating a feathery haze in the pasture and into the mountain's crevices.

"How was the cruise?" Tom's voice came from the barn.

Ruthanne jumped and slipped away from Skye. "What are you still doing here?"

"You had some lightbulbs out in the yard, so I replaced them after the feeding."

"Thanks. I kept meaning to tell you about them."

"You should have come with us," Skye said.

"I've already been on that cruise. Speedboats freak me out, and I don't need that kind of abuse." Since big Tom could admit that so freely, Skye decided he'd cut Paul some slack.

After Tom left them standing by Lirit's pen, Skye drew Ruthanne into his arms and tasted her lips once more. She returned his love with silent promises, but when they parted, she seemed pensive.

"What's wrong?" He hoped she was only tired from the full day of recreation.

She smiled up at him, placing another brief kiss on his mouth. "Nothing. I'm thinking about my talk with Paul."

He released her. "You're thinking about Paul while kissing me?"

"No, silly." She beat his chest with all the fury of a kitten at play. "Well, not exactly. I told him I didn't feel a future with him was in God's will. Then I told him how I gauged that. I think you should know, too."

As she explained Lirit's hum of contentment, Skye looked with wonder at the supposedly dumb beast that helped Ruthanne listen to her own heart. The alpaca, having heard her name, pushed against the gate to be near her owner.

"You know"—Skye motioned with his eyes toward their subject—"I've never heard Lirit hum when she's content, only when she's stressing like the other animals." He rubbed his chin. "In fact, she never seems content around me. Like she's mad at me or something."

Ruthanne stroked Lirit's neck. "That's absurd. She's the gentlest alpaca on the ranch."

"Whatever." He jerked his chin toward the beast. "When it's just her and me, she either spits or sulks in a corner."

Ruthanne cocked her head and looked Lirit in the eye. "Maybe she senses our attraction to each other."

Skye pondered that statement for a moment. He wasn't sure he believed Lirit was jealous, but she seemed to get some kind of vibe from him. *God's will*. Could she sense his bitterness toward his mother?

With their chores finished, Skye kissed Ruthanne good night then walked back to the house.

Straight to his mother's bedroom door.

fourteen

Skye grasped the doorknob and slowly turned it. He almost expected beaded curtains on the windows and the stale-sweet odor of incense-saturated fabric to assault his nose. But this room reflected the taste of the rest of the house. Handcrafted wooden furniture and soft colors of various earth hues in the bedspread and drapes shocked him more than the psychedelic colors his mother used to love.

Her guitar sat perched in an old wooden rocker near the bed, nestled artfully among the soft billows of a knitted afghan. He picked it up and sat on the edge of the bed, manipulating his fingers into the one chord she'd taught him. Was it an A? The *plunk* of his fingertips against the three strings sounded just as childlike as when he was young.

Setting the guitar aside, he remembered how his mother always kept a peach-scented talc pouch in the tiny compartment inside the case. He loved that smell. Sometimes he'd ask her to play just so she would take the pouch out, dry her fingers with it, and hand it to him to hold. He found the case behind the rocker, laid it on the bed, and opened it. The scent wafted toward him, which immediately threw his mind into memories. The gold felt interior was still in good condition, and the tiny compartment that held guitar picks and small items still had the ribbon sewn on to open it. He grasped it and flipped the lid up, knowing the pouch of talc would be inside. It was, lying on top of a photograph.

His fingers tightened into a fist before he relaxed them enough to pick up the photo for a better look. His young mother smiled into the camera, her long blond hair in motion as if a small breeze had decided to play with the fine strands. Unexpected emotion rose up within him, like a parched flower receiving a long-needed watering. He had loved this woman so much. He knew the little boy with her was himself. What was he, about seven years old? He wore a blue cowboy hat and sat astride one of six horses tied to a central hub. This looked like the pony rides at the county fair.

Skye had to wring out his brain to extract the memory. His dad wasn't in the picture, so was he behind the camera? No, he didn't come with them that day. A tight knot grabbed Skye's stomach. They had gone to the fair without his dad, and when they returned, they found he had died of an overdose. That hadn't bothered Skye as much as his mother's hysterical reaction. No wonder he had chosen to forget that day.

But now it came flooding in. They were going to attend the fair as a family, but that morning his dad refused to go, choosing instead to stay with his friends and their funny pipes. Mom was furious. She didn't know how to drive and had no way to get there. Then a man from the commune offered to take them. Skye liked this man better than he ever liked his dad. He often sat with Skye when his parents were away or incapacitated. He bought him that hat.

Suddenly tired, Skye curled up on the bed, the photo pressed to his chest. With his mother's guitar on the rocker the last thing he saw before closing his eyes, he spent the night dreaming of the good times.

❧

Ruthanne's humming heart woke her before her alarm had a chance. Both Skye and Paul now knew about her gauge for God's will. Her confession made it seem all the more valid. With fresh excitement she looked forward to seeing Skye.

Even so, she decided to drop by Lirit's pen for some girl talk before going into the main house.

"Last night I prayed that God would work things out

between Skye and Hannie," she confided as Lirit munched hay. "It was a selfish prayer, I admit. I want to pursue our relationship free of guilt and anxiety. Peace settled in my heart. I just know that all will be well. Hannie will wake up, and she and Skye will talk. They'll set their differences aside, and we can all move forward."

She expected the low droning hum that came so easily to Lirit, but instead her ears flattened and an ugly snort rippled her mouth, spewing wet bits of hay.

"Really, Lirit. Why don't you like him? You know I'd never let a man come between us." She reached out to pet the woolly neck, but Lirit sidestepped out of reach. Ruthanne pulled her hand back and pressed it to her chest. "Do you know something I don't?"

A chill settled in her heart, snuffing out the peace she'd felt last night.

As she entered the main house, dark and empty, an unbidden thought caused her heart to lurch. Where was Skye? Had he left her, just like Brian did? She rebuked that notion, demanding that it not rule over her anymore. She was tired of fearing the worst from men and from Skye in particular. He was not Brian and had proved himself many times over.

She flicked the light switch on in the kitchen, and it illuminated a handwritten note on the table.

"R, I'm sorry to bail on you today. My sister called early this morning. Her car broke down on her way to school, and she called me in a panic. Women! Ha-ha (sorry). Anyway, I need to tow her home, and then I have to fix this thing once and for all. I hope to be back later for the evening feeding, but I'll call you if I get tied up. Love, S."

Disappointment washed over her, then she chided herself for acting like a fifteen-year-old with a crush. However, that didn't stop her from reading his bold handwriting again and focusing on the end of his note—"*Love, S*".

With a spring in her step and the memory of his tender kisses, she headed out to the barn to start the round of feeding. A love song bubbled up from her heart, and she found herself whistling it while tossing chicken feed out to the gathering brood.

"You sound happy."

"Hi, Tom. It's a beautiful day." She tried to act as nonchalant as possible but knew her burning cheeks gave her away.

He glanced around. "Where's your counterpart?"

"A small family emergency—car trouble."

Tom's face fell, and he looked as disappointed as she had felt earlier. "We were going to finish the barn."

"Give me an hour, and I'll help you."

He winked. "You're on."

She breezed through the feeding while Tom hauled water to the troughs, then they worked together preparing to paint the entire barn wall.

"Why can't we just paint over the damaged part?" Ruthanne stirred red paint in the five-gallon bucket, looking dubiously at the other three Tom had left in a corner. "This seems like so much."

"We can't just paint the new part of the barn because it won't match. The whole wall has to be painted for continuity, and if the rest of the barn doesn't look right, we'll have to paint the whole thing."

Ruthanne winced. "What is this costing us?"

"Nothing. Skye's insurance is paying for all the repairs." Tom hauled out the ladder. "So, you didn't tell me last night. What did you think of the cruise? Did you have fun?"

Ruthanne hesitated. Paul was no fun at first. But the memory of Skye's soft lips on hers was quite enjoyable.

"Well? You did go, didn't you?"

"What? Yes." Daydreaming on the job. And—oh swell!—now she had a red paint splotch on her shoe. "I had a great time."

Tom stopped halfway up the ladder and grinned. "What aren't you telling me? Maybe I should rephrase. Did you have fun with Skye?"

"Am I that transparent?" Or had Tom seen their hand-holding last night?

He wrapped his arm around a rung and scratched his nose. "Girlie, other than Hannie or her nephew, I probably know you better than anyone. I may be dumb, but I got eyes." He pointed with two fingers at his eyeballs. "And these peepers tell me you've got feelings for the new guy."

She had no words. He'd summed it up concisely, so she merely nodded.

Tom took another step up and chuckled. "Then you'd better brush up on your Old West trivia."

☙

"Okay, if you won't junk this thing, I will," Skye mumbled from under the hood of Robyn's cute but failing sports car.

"You taught me to be frugal, big bro." She leaned over the fender to peer at the partially dismantled engine. "And besides, I don't get paid enough to buy a new car."

He turned to look at her. His gorgeous youngest sister had been working hard to pay off her student loans. Skye was proud of her, but enough was enough.

After wiping his hands on an oily rag, he pointed to the engine and pretended to shoot it. "That's what they did in the Old West when their horses couldn't take another step." He palmed his chest over his heart. "It's the humane way."

Robyn flipped her strawberry-colored ponytail and jabbed her finger into his chest. "Are you telling me you can't fix it?"

He started loading up his tools. "Get out the shovel, and bury the old girl." He pinched her chin, purposely leaving a dark smudge. "Go wash your face. I'll drive you to work."

He felt lighter than he had for years. For the first time, he started to feel the puzzle pieces of his life come together.

Now if he could only talk to his birth mother. After all the great things he'd heard about her, she must have had a good reason for not contacting him sooner, and he prayed he'd get the chance to ask her about it.

The radio in his parents' garage was blasting contemporary Christian music. As he put the tools away, he barely heard his cell phone ring. It was Paul.

"I just spoke to the doctor. He plans to bring Aunt Hannie out of the coma this afternoon. Her lungs are healing nicely, so he feels it's time."

"How long will it take?" Skye glanced at his watch. "I have to get my sister to school and then go back to the ranch to change."

"Take your time getting here. The doc said after they're out of the coma it usually takes awhile for the patient to wake up naturally."

Skye promised to get there as soon as he could and prompted Robyn to hurry up.

He arrived back at the ranch within an hour. Ruthanne had already left for the hospital. Between fixing Robyn's car and rushing back to the ranch, Skye had missed lunch. He opened the refrigerator, but the contents morphed into a vision of his mother lying comatose in the hospital bed. Would he finally get to talk to her? The coolness from the refrigerator suddenly chilled him clear through. How she answered his *why* question could impact his budding romance with Ruthanne. His appetite gone, he squeezed his eyes shut and leaned on the still-open door. "Please, God. Give me strength."

Without grabbing a thing to eat, he headed out. When he arrived at the hospital, nausea swirled in his empty stomach. He reprimanded himself for allowing his nerves to dictate his common sense.

Ruthanne greeted him in the visitors' lounge then stepped

into his embrace. "I'm so glad you're here." She wrapped her arms around his neck. He drew strength from her touch, grateful that God had brought her into his life, if only for the moment when he talked to his mother for the first time.

Paul sat in the corner, his legs and arms crossed while he watched a news channel on the small television hanging in the corner.

Dr. Harris entered and sat down with the three of them. His white coat contrasted sharply with his African-American skin. He spoke with professionalism, but his eyes held compassion. "We've stopped the drug therapy, and tests indicate that she's out of the coma. It's all up to her now. Her lungs are strong, so I'm confident she'll pull through all of this."

A voice from the speaker overhead paged his name, and he stood. "Are there any more questions?"

Ruthanne motioned with her hand. "Can we sit with her so she's not alone when she wakes up?"

"Certainly. I think that's a great idea."

Panic rose in Skye's throat. Could he sit in her room for that long? Mentally pulling himself up by his bootstraps, he decided to be strong.

But as they all walked to the room, the little boy inside him tried to dig in his heels, making Skye's size elevens feel like lead.

fifteen

As always, Ruthanne felt drawn to Hannie's side by their invisible bond. Paul followed closely, but Skye tagged behind by several yards. She knew he had never made it all the way into the room, usually choosing to hang out at the doorjamb, but today she decided to help him.

When he showed up at the door, she held out her hand. Warmth spread through her as he stepped inside and joined her. She did notice, however, that he had trouble looking at Hannie.

She squeezed his palm and gazed up at him. "What is it? Talk to me."

"It's hard to envision this woman as the young mom I remember."

Ruthanne caught Paul's glance across the bed. She was sure they wondered the same thing: Would they find out what happened?

When Skye didn't volunteer the information, Ruthanne took a deep breath as she tested their new bond. "Would you like to talk about it?"

He stepped away from the bed but this time didn't flee out the door. He lowered himself into one of the three chairs a nurse had graciously maneuvered into the tiny space. "Let me talk to her first." He balled his fists and pressed them into the arm of the chair. "I'd like to tell you everything, but I'd rather do it with grace, and right now I don't feel that."

She lowered herself into the chair next to him. "I understand. Whenever you're ready." *Please, God, make him ready soon.*

Paul still stood by the bed, fidgeting with the sheet, tucking it neatly around his aunt. Then he stroked her hand. Ruthanne praised God for this compassionate man.

Lord, bring someone into Paul's life who will laugh at his wit, lean on his strength, and love him beyond anything he could imagine.

She tried to picture the girl God would send to Paul. Petite, feminine, an appreciator of gourmet food. She would laugh at all his jokes, love all his quirks, and be a gentle helpmate.

It was almost as if she were penning a want ad. Would God send a sweet Mary Poppins as a result? Ruthanne tried to suppress a giggle.

With a cocked eyebrow, Paul regarded her. She felt grateful he hadn't heard her silly prayer.

He looked back at Hannie. "She looks different somehow. As if before she wasn't really in there, but now she is. Yet she hasn't moved."

Ruthanne nodded. "I see it, too." In fact it looked as if she would awaken at any moment.

But she didn't. Afternoon gave way to evening, and soon they were turning on lights in the darkening room.

Skye glanced at his watch and sat up straight. "Should I go feed the animals?"

"No," Ruthanne answered. "Tom said he'd take care of things while we were gone."

His stomach rumbled, and Ruthanne turned to him. "When did you eat last?"

His blue eyes widened. "Was it that obvious?"

Paul lounged with his leg over the arm of his chair on the far side of the bed. "Hey, I heard it from here."

Ruthanne leaned forward. "Okay, executive-decision time. Why don't you two go get some dinner and bring something back for me?"

"I have a better idea." Paul motioned toward the door. "Why don't you two go have dinner? I ate a late lunch while waiting for you both to come to the hospital."

Ruthanne believed the excuse but also knew this was Paul's way of saying he took their conversation during the cruise seriously. He was willing to be just friends, and his offer was his way of blessing her relationship with Skye. "Okay but we'll consider this the first watch since it seems we'll be sitting with her through the night."

Skye reached for her hand, sending a thrill through her at his touch. "I'll take the second watch so Ruthanne can get some rest." He stood and pulled her to her feet. "If you drag the waiting room chairs out there together to make a bed, they're probably a step down from crippling."

Ruthanne laughed. "Don't try writing publicity copy." She glanced at Paul. "Sounds like a plan. We'll bring you back dinner though."

"Whatever. That's fine."

As a tribute to his selflessness, she tossed up one last request on his behalf. *And have this Mary Poppins want to spoil him thoroughly.*

ঌ

The hospital cafeteria had already closed, so Skye and Ruthanne found a small café nearby. He enjoyed the small talk, carefully sidestepping any conversation about his mother. He wanted to tell Ruthanne everything but felt the temper of that conversation hinged on what he would learn from the stranger in the hospital bed. If his mother could explain her actions thirty-eight years ago in a way that made sense, then he could speak about it with Ruthanne in a civil—yes, even celebratory—manner. But if the conversation went horribly wrong, he would have no good words to say and would probably alienate Ruthanne. She, along with the rest of the world, had placed his mother on a pedestal. Ruthanne would probably fight to keep her there.

Once the meal was over, they ordered takeout for Paul and

headed back to the hospital where Skye took the next watch.

The night nurse came in and felt for his mother's pulse, looked at readouts on the machine, and changed a bag hanging on a pole. She glanced at him then back to what she was doing. "Are you the son?"

"Yes."

"Well, I'm sure she'll be happy to see you when she wakes up."

He nodded, but he wasn't so sure. Now that he was facing an evening alone with her, the enemy had been barraging him again with lies that made sense. *You're worthless. Your own mother tried to get rid of you.* He pulled his pocket Bible out, and the voice sizzled away, like a hot fire doused with cool water.

The nurse spoke again. "I'll bring you a pillow and blanket."

"Thank you."

For most of his shift he flipped through his Bible, reading about vulnerable men who became mighty in the Lord. Joseph, David, Gideon, all with real problems in their lives, some bigger than the giant Goliath. Some as intense as questioning faith. God never let them down, and their strength of character became their legacy.

He closed his eyes. *Lord, I confess that my faith is small right now. The pain is so real. How can my mother make everything right again? Gideon tested You with a fleece. Dry when there was dew on the ground then again wet if no dew was present. I, also, lay a fleece before You. If, when my mother awakes, she indicates no joy at my presence, doesn't reach out for me, I'll walk away and continue my life as before. Amen.*

Oddly peace eluded him after that prayer.

As night swallowed the little room and the nurses began speaking in hushed voices at their station near the door, the words in Skye's Bible blurred then disappeared one by one. He awoke, startled as the book hit the floor. When he retrieved it and stood to stretch, he glanced over at the bed. Instead of a sleeping form, he saw his mother's blue eyes trained on him.

Eyes that he had at one time longed to see again but then had haunted his dreams until only a few years ago.

He blinked back stinging tears. Tucking the Bible into his breast pocket, he shifted to stand by the bed. The eyes followed him. "It's me." His voice cracked. "It's me, Skye."

She didn't smile. She didn't reach out. She only stared. Remembering his prayer, the seven-year-old within wanted to reach out and shake her. Knowing that would do no good, he tore out of the room as the accusing voice in his head cackled with delight.

≈

A sharp pain in her neck woke Ruthanne. Skye had used the word *crippling* when referring to the chairs in the waiting room. He was right. Her gaze sought out Paul in the dim room, sleeping like a newborn cria. He could have at least looked uncomfortable for her sake.

A window faced east where a crimson sliver of light peeked between the slats of the vinyl blinds. She glanced at her watch in alarm then hopped out of the improvised bed as fast as her twisted body would let her. She'd missed her shift.

Where was Skye? Had he fallen asleep? When she reached the room, she peered in. Only Hannie, lying in the same position she'd left her in last night.

With a hand on her hip, she tried to convince herself that Skye had just lost track of time. He probably took a break and hadn't made it back to the waiting room. She glanced both ways down the corridor. No Skye, but a nurse approached her sporting a friendly smile. "Mrs. Godfrey woke up about five hours ago."

"She did?" Ruthanne glanced at the sleeping form, selfishly wishing she'd been the one on watch. "Was Skye with her?"

"Her son? Yes, but only for a moment." She entered the room to check Hannie's pulse. "He let us know at the nurses' station, then he left."

"He left?" Ruthanne rubbed her aching neck. "Where?"

The nurse continued her routine attention to Hannie, apparently too busy to see Ruthanne's confusion. "I don't know. He did ask one of the other nurses to wake you. But then we had an emergency with another patient down the hall. I guess in our busyness no one came to get you."

"No, they didn't." She walked over to Hannie. "She's asleep again?"

"Yes, she'll do that for a little while, wake and sleep. With each interval she'll become more aware." She smiled. "You'd think she'd have rested enough, but for some reason that's not the case."

As the nurse left, she offered her a cup of coffee or tea, which Ruthanne refused.

Her stomach roiled. Why did Skye leave—again? Did Hannie somehow upset him? He seemed on edge last night, but after he agreed to stay with Hannie for several hours, Ruthanne thought he was okay.

The man sure had a habit of taking off. After what her husband had put her through, she certainly didn't need that again.

Remembering the real reason she was there, she put her anger on hold. With one last check on Hannie, Ruthanne noticed something different. A single salty tear track from the corner of her eye to the pillow.

Paul entered yawning, looking like a child with his mussed hair and crumpled clothes. "They just told me Aunt Hannie woke up." He went to Hannie's side but didn't take her hand like he'd always done before. "Is she asleep again?"

"Yes, but the nurse said she'll wake up again and with each time stay awake longer."

After she filled him in on Skye, he asked, "Did you try to call his cell?"

She hadn't thought of that. How could Paul be so logical

when he first woke up? "No. I'll do that now." She pulled her phone out of her purse and called but only got his voice mail. After leaving a brief message, her irritation with Skye gave way to alarm. "I hope he's okay."

"Look." Paul sank into the chair and raked his fingers through the dark tangles on his head. "He's a grown man and a dedicated Christian. I'm sure it was very hard for him to see his mom for the first time after so many years. Give him time. He's probably off praying by himself."

Ruthanne nodded, wishing Skye would include her in his pain.

&

Even while Skye fled back to the ranch, he wondered what he was doing. It was as if something had taken possession of him and he was powerless to stop it.

Thirty days was apparently not enough time to get to know his mother through her friends. Everything he had learned about her dissolved when she woke up and never even smiled. He expected some kind of warmth but only got that same listless stare he remembered when she was high.

He pulled into the ranch drive and stalked toward the house. As of today his obligation was over. He had planned to pack later, but now he threw everything into his suitcase and went outside to retrieve his dog.

Tom was in the far paddock feeding the alpacas. He hadn't seen Skye, and that was okay. It would only lead to more talk about his mother.

He loaded Ruddy into the SUV and sped out of there, anxious to put some distance between him and his past. The paradox, however, was that Ruthanne held his future.

He couldn't think of that right now. Too much baggage lay between them, and he knew he must address it before he could offer her the kind of love she deserved.

Then why, he asked himself, was he running?

He didn't know. He also didn't understand why, instead of getting off the interstate to go home, he found himself plowing ahead, not knowing where he might land.

After passing Merrick, he tried to envision his troubles flying out the open windows. He turned on the radio to silence the voice of reason telling him to turn back, but static poured out.

With a flat palm, he smacked the steering wheel. "Great! A wire must have come loose." He slapped the dash, trying to jar it back into place.

Alone with his thoughts, he found himself jealous of carefree Ruddy leaning out the window, the breeze whipping his tongue to his right cheek.

As Skye's adrenaline finally dissipated, he realized he'd driven halfway to Eugene. The car nearly exited itself off the highway, and it was only then that he realized his destination.

Before long, the River Bend Cabins came into view. He had often spent time there with his family for fishing and rafting trips. Yes, this would be a great place to get his thoughts in order. Perhaps if he immersed himself in the positive memories, he could better handle the crazy turn his life had taken the past thirty days.

Since it was the end of the off-season, he had no trouble renting a cabin. After a quick trip to a tiny market up the road, he had enough provisions to last a week, plus a fishing pole and flies. By nightfall he and Ruddy had dined on hot dogs and potato chips and he'd wet his fishing line in the Umpqua River that ran only a few yards from his door.

❧

"I'm sorry to drag you out here, Mrs. Randall, but I'm so worried about Skye."

"Please, call me Cynthia. And it was my choice to come to you."

"Thank you." Ruthanne nodded and blinked back tears.

Ruthanne's concern for Skye heightened when she'd gone

home briefly yesterday and noticed that all his things were gone. The familiar panic came rushing in. Brian had left the same way. She called Mrs. Randall who graciously agreed to meet her at the hospital.

The two women found a quiet corner in the waiting room.

"How is Hannah?"

"She's in and out but can't move yet because her muscles have atrophied. Even a smile is impossible right now. But they'll launch into therapy soon."

"I'd like to see her before I leave. I've never met her, of course."

"The Hannie I know would be very pleased." Of course there was that other Hannie who still mystified Ruthanne. "But first I'd like to talk about Skye." Another person who mystified her. "Does he have a habit of running? I want to understand him, but these disappearing acts are beyond me." Her voice cracked.

Cynthia pulled a tissue from her purse and handed it to Ruthanne. "When he first came to us, he wandered away whenever the mood struck him. I think after living in a commune he had been used to coming and going as he pleased."

Ruthanne, who had been dabbing her eyes, jerked her head up from the tissue. "Skye lived in a commune?"

Cynthia sat back in the chair and crossed her legs. She seemed to be thinking—or possibly praying—about her next words. "Skye and his mother have put you through a lot this past month. I feel you have a right to know some things." She took a deep breath. "Yes, from what he could tell us, that's what we gathered. Skye's parents were hippies, and they lived with several other people. Skye's father wanted little to do with him, but Hannie did love her son. . .as much as she was capable of. He talks of her singing to him and taking him places. But what confused him as a young child was how she could completely ignore him at times. This happened, of course, when she was taking drugs."

Ruthanne squeezed her eyes shut. Brian's addiction to alcohol had eventually led in the same direction. She never wanted to deal with that again. Knowing now what a dangerous situation Skye had been in, she felt a new compassion for him. "Was he abused?"

Cynthia frowned. "He only has one mark in the center of his back. It looks like someone put out a cigarette there."

Ruthanne gulped back her revulsion. She'd never seen Skye with his shirt off, even when the day grew warm and sweat stains were evident.

"As Skye opened up, we learned that some of the men mistreated him. Hannie protected him when she could, but other times. . ."

"She was incapacitated."

"That's what we assume, especially after Skye's father died."

"Were there other children in the commune?"

"He talked about younger children, so he must have been the first to be born in their group. I don't know what happened to the others, but I've prayed they found their ways into good homes."

"So. . ." Ruthanne tried to recap what she'd just learned so her brain could catch up. "He is prone to wandering when distressed, but he won't hurt himself and he'll come back." *He'll come back.*

Cynthia nodded, the peaceful look on her face indicative of the trust she'd placed in her son.

She leaned forward and wrapped her warm hands around Ruthanne's own. Without asking permission, she closed her eyes and launched into a heartfelt prayer that brought the tears back to Ruthanne's eyes.

"Father God, please speak to Skye wherever he is. His soul is hurting, but I know You've brought his mother back into his life for healing. Speak to his heart. Help him forgive."

She then prayed for Hannie and lastly for Ruthanne to be at peace and to trust God.

When Ruthanne looked up, she saw a mist of tears in the other woman's eyes. This was a mother who ached because her son ached.

The cheerful strains of the song "Blue Skies" drifted from Cynthia's purse. "That's Skye." She flashed a proud mom smile. "It's our special song." When she answered her cell phone, Ruthanne marveled at her grace. "Hi, honey. Long time no see. Do you have something to tell me?"

By her half of the conversation, Ruthanne surmised that Skye was okay.

"You're where?. . . Oh, that's a beautiful place!. . . Caught anything?" There was a longer pause. "Yes, I'm at the hospital visiting with her right now. . . . Okay, I'll tell her. . . . Love you, too. Bye."

She slipped the phone back into her purse. "He's fine. There's a little place halfway between here and Eugene where he can pray and reflect."

"And fish, I assume."

Again the invigorating laugh put Ruthanne at ease. "Never underestimate the power of a good fishing hole. I have faith that he will get through this. . .and come back to you."

Ruthanne's cheeks grew warm. "Me?"

Without explaining she went on. "He wanted me to tell you not to worry and to thank you for all you've done for him."

"What have I done?"

"He didn't tell me."

sixteen

The small Bible felt heavy in Skye's denim shirt pocket. As he sat on a boulder near the river, he confessed that he'd done more fishing than praying in the last few days. His pole now lay beside him, the line still dry. He'd broken away from his reality to be alone with the Lord, and now he had to make good on that promise.

Ruddy had chased a squirrel under a boulder, and the rodent chattered at him from an escape hatch on the other side. Skye attempted to ignore the squabble as he prayed. "Lord, You know what I've been through. Up until my adoption, I had a lousy childhood. And I had pretty much gotten past that when my mother drew me back into her life. Why have You done this to me?"

The rushing river nearly hypnotized him as he gazed at the rocks dancing deep below the surface. But the movement was only an illusion.

Had his life been an illusion? From the time he settled into his adoptive family to the time his mother sought him out, he realized now he'd been living a double life. Outwardly all was well. He loved his parents and sisters. He did well in school and gladly followed his dad into the family business. And yet he harbored a deep, dark secret. He hated his birth mother. And as each year passed with no contact from her, that current of hate dug itself deeper and deeper into the silt until not even a ripple disturbed his smoothly flowing life.

He picked up a flat stone and hurled it into the water, not even attempting to make it skip. It sank into the hidden currents, and his mind landed there, too—to the dark ugliness he had hidden so well. While others were praising him for being such a good boy, he knew he wasn't.

And he hated himself for it. So many times he asked God to forgive him for his dark thoughts, but he never felt peace.

He finally pulled the Bible from his pocket and started to thumb through it. At first nothing he read applied to him. He'd never been one to open his Bible and stab a finger at random pages, but that's what he did now, flipping through book after book, chapter after chapter, in hopes that a verse would bold and magnify itself on the page.

And then it happened. The page flipped to a passage in Mark where his eyes caught the word "forgive" used twice in one sentence. *"And when you stand praying, if you hold anything against anyone, forgive him, so that your Father in heaven may forgive you your sins."*

He must have read that before.

He read it again with the surrounding verses. They talked about mountain-moving faith—if you don't doubt, it will be given to you.

At that moment, he knew forgiveness eluded him not only because of his deep-seated rage against his mother but because he doubted God could ever forgive him for his hypocrisy.

He grabbed another rock. Could forgiveness be as easy as releasing a stone into the river? The hard, cold object weighted his hand as his fingers wrapped around it. He closed his eyes, and in words foreign to his own ears, he said, "I forgive my mother." Then he skipped the stone. It skimmed the water once before disappearing.

With another rock he prayed, "I forgive my mother for not standing up for me when others abused me." The released rock skimmed twice.

"I forgive my mother for neglecting me." The third rock skimmed several times.

He continued this ritual until every issue but one had been

satisfied. He felt lighter, but the one question still burned deep in his heart.

Why?

The invisible nudging at his back was as tangible as the last stone in his hand. He gripped it tightly, not willing to release it.

"I can't, Lord. I can't stop wondering why she left me. I can't stop. . .hating her for leaving me!"

"If you hold anything against anyone, forgive him, so that your Father in heaven may forgive you your sins."

Knowing he'd never realize true freedom until he threw that last rock, he squared his shoulders and pitched it with all his might. "I forgive my mother for. . .for leaving me."

The stone skipped seven times over the ripples, a new record for Skye.

An overwhelming sense of release lifted his heavy heart as the burden he had carried for so many years skipped away with the stone. He heard a bird warbling a tune, and the joyful sound orchestrated the music bubbling in his soul. Refreshing tears filled his eyes as he looked to the sky.

"Thank You, Lord."

Before leaving that day, he gathered several more rocks as an altar, commemorating the day he released his anger into the river.

❧

"Look at you." Ruthanne walked into Hannie's new hospital room, happy to see her surrounded by a cheerier motif than the cold, white ICU room she'd been in for the past two months. A swirled mauve and blue pattern on the wall facing her bed seemed to encourage the patient to gain strength. With the ventilator removed, the tube in her throat no longer hindered her.

Hannie's eyes lit up, cheering Ruthanne's heart. She still couldn't lift her arms, but her smile had returned. Ruthanne grasped her hand, praying for the day her fingers would squeeze back.

"Daughter." Her raspy speech shocked Ruthanne. The tube must have irritated her throat.

"Hey." Ruthanne blinked back tears. "You're going to make me cry. It's an honor to be considered your daughter."

"Oh no, not that again." Paul sauntered in, his hands in his pockets. "Hi, Auntie." He took his position on the other side of the bed and began massaging her hand. "It's been nonstop waterworks around here ever since you woke up."

"It has not." Ruthanne wanted to throw something at him, but everything within reach was either too heavy or screwed to the floor. She had just started eyeing one of Hannie's dozens of potted plants lined on the windowsill when she noticed Paul shifting uncomfortably.

Hannie seemed to be signaling Paul with her eyes. He glanced at Ruthanne, and she instantly knew Hannie was asking how their relationship was going. The poor woman was still playing matchmaker.

Both Ruthanne and Paul dropped their gazes to the floor. When Ruthanne looked back at her, a frown had creased Hannie's forehead.

In a retreat maneuver, Ruthanne told her how the craft fair went and about the new crias that had been born in the last month. She was gearing up to tell her how Skye had done on the ranch when the subject himself showed up at the door.

One foot in and one foot out.

Ruthanne raised her hand to him, and he walked boldly into the room.

⁂

Ruthanne's hand felt cool in Skye's palm, but her grip left a clear message: *You're not going to run again, buster.* When he smiled at her and squeezed back, she relaxed considerably.

He praised God. Gone was the child who had internally

kicked and screamed whenever he crossed the threshold. In his place was a man determined to keep that mountain moved.

His mother watched the exchange then smiled. A small smile but definitely more than the expression on her face a few days ago. Expecting his anger to rise at the memory, Skye exhaled a relieved breath when it didn't, thanking God for silencing the voice in his head.

Letting go of Ruthanne's hand, he knew he could do the next thing by himself.

He reached for his mother's hand and held it in both of his own.

She swallowed hard. "Skye." Her scratchy voice seemed to irritate her. Skye leaned down where she could whisper in his ear. "Forgive me."

All Skye ever wanted was to know *why*. However, new God-inspired words slipped from his lips. "I forgive you."

Somewhere behind him, he heard Ruthanne sniffle. Paul, who'd been standing on the other side, almost in protective mode, released Hannie's other hand and backed away.

Skye gazed into his mother's tear-brimmed eyes, blue like his own, then bent down and kissed her cheek.

❧

Ruthanne snatched several tissues from the box by Hannie's bed. Just as she was about to blow her nose, she heard a large honk that sounded like a goose had been released into the hallway. Tom stood at the door, wiping his red nose with a handkerchief. His eyes shone bright.

Hannie's eyes trained on him. They seemed to draw him near, and he took the side of the bed that Paul had just vacated. Ruthanne glanced around the room. Paul had disappeared.

She was about to slip out also when Skye captured her hand. Wondering if he needed her strength, she joined him. But once she made the connection with him, she sensed he didn't need her but wanted to include her. She had to still her singing heart so she could hear the conversation taking place.

Tom was explaining Hannie's medical condition to Skye. ". . .and with her in the coma so long, her muscles have forgotten how to work."

Skye glanced at Hannie. "So that's why you didn't react to me that first night." He closed his eyes and drew in a sharp breath. "I'm an idiot."

"The doc says she'll have to go through tons of therapy, but she will get all her faculties back."

In answer Skye raised Hannie's hand and kissed it. Ruthanne remembered what his adoptive mother had said about his childhood and breathed a quick prayer of thanks that he had apparently found peace while away.

Hannie's eyes turned sorrowful. "The park."

Ruthanne felt Skye stiffen. Hannie frowned, touched the bandage at her throat, then looked at Tom. With more force than she'd had a moment ago, she said, "Tell him."

Tom shifted his feet. He clearly did not want to be the one having this conversation. "I'm sure you remember the commune. Do you remember losing your dad? The way he died?"

Skye nodded.

"Well, after that, Hannie fell apart completely."

Questions darted in Ruthanne's mind. How did Tom know these things? Had Hannie opened up to him? Why hadn't she told her? She tamped down the confusing jealousy, realizing there was more at stake in the small room than her feelings.

Tom continued. "She could barely control her drug habit when he was alive, but afterward. . .it was a wonder that she didn't die, too." He rubbed his nose, as if he felt uncomfortable speaking for someone else. "I don't know what she was thinking, but she got it in her head to take you with her when she met her supplier. There was a park nearby, and she told you to play on the swings until she came back."

"But she didn't."

Skye squeezed Ruthanne's fingers, and she fought not to cry out.

"No. She forgot where she put you." Tom paused, letting that sink in for a moment. "By the time she was cognitive enough to remember, she learned on a news report that you had already been found by the police."

"It was best," Hannie rasped.

Skye shook his head. "No, a child belongs with his mother."

For the first time, Hannie shook her head ever so slightly. "They would have killed you."

Ruthanne gasped. What horrors had this woman and her child been forced to endure? She suspected Skye's adoptive mom hadn't told her everything about the commune full of drugged men who abused Skye. Perhaps she didn't know it all herself.

"Hannie." Ruthanne ran her fingers through her friend's hair. "Why didn't you tell me?"

Hannie squeezed her eyes shut. "Ashamed."

Tom spoke to Skye again. "She was in pain for a long time over her decision not to find you. I'd like to tell you that she buckled down and beat her addiction, just so she could get you back. But it only got worse. It was four long years before she came out of it."

Hannie's sorrow-filled eyes suddenly gleamed. "God did it."

Tom glanced down at her with affection. "Yes. God grabbed hold of her and wouldn't let go. Right, Hannie? A street missionary gave her a Bible, and she pored over it while in detox. It took a lot of strength on her part, but eventually she never had to go back."

"After she became sober," Skye asked, "why didn't she come for me?" He glanced at Hannie. "I found out that you've known where I was all this time."

Tears trickled down her cheeks. Skye took a tissue and dabbed awkwardly at them.

Tom continued for her. "It took her awhile to get back on her feet. She married David, and by the time she was at the place to bring you back into her life, you were doing very well. You'd landed with people who loved you. Why mess with that?"

Skye folded himself into the armchair. "Wow."

"I know." Tom nodded. "It's a lot to take in."

Ruthanne couldn't be still any longer. "Tom, how do you know all this?"

He drew in a big breath. "I lived in the commune with Hannie and Skye."

Skye suddenly stood and searched Tom's face.

"When Hannie and her new husband found me in prison," Tom continued, "she swore me to secrecy. She'd begun a new life, and her friends didn't need to know what she'd done."

"Did David know?" Ruthanne asked. Skye was trembling next to her.

"Yes. She filled him in on everything." Tom rubbed his nose and took on a sheepish look. He lifted his hand and wiggled his fingers in a tiny wave directed at Skye. "Hi, little Destry."

seventeen

"You were the nice man in the commune?"

"Guilty." Tom raised his hand.

Ruthanne watched Skye turn from an adult to a child of seven. His feet seemed to move of their own volition. He rounded the end of the bed and met Tom on the other side where the two embraced.

"You made my life bearable." Skye's emotion-filled voice sounded muffled against the larger man's shoulder.

Tom patted his back, blinking away his own tears. "You needed a dad. I needed someone to care for. It just worked out."

When they finally parted, Ruthanne sensed a deep scar had been healed within Skye.

The two reminisced for a few minutes, mostly Tom filling in the blanks of Skye's memory. Then, after another hug that included slaps on their backs, Skye sat on the side of the bed, his left leg in half-Indian style, as close to Hannie as possible. He draped his arm lazily over one knee and filled her in on his life.

Ruthanne drank in the scene before her, the scar in her own heart beginning to soften.

As Hannie gazed with contentment at her son, it was evident how much stress she'd been under. With it gone, she looked beautiful from within.

After snatching another couple of tissues, Ruthanne signaled Tom with her eyebrows, silently asking if they should leave. He nodded and wiped his own nose with his handkerchief. They both left without disturbing the reunion.

They entered the waiting area and sat down. A brief glance

told her that Paul was nowhere around. Now that Skye had taken on his rightful role as Hannie's son, had Paul felt unneeded in the room?

She glanced at Tom as a comfortable silence stretched between them.

"So. . ." Tom scratched the side of his nose. "Now you know. I guess we can praise God even in her illness. If she hadn't gotten sick, she may never have had the courage to seek Skye out."

"And none of this would have come to light." Ruthanne massaged her temples. "Poor Hannie. So many years of grief yet knowing she'd made the right decision."

"Well, the right decision would have been not to put her child in that position in the first place. But I'm the last person to judge on that score."

Sensing his need for comfort, she reached out to touch his hand. "I've always been proud of you, Tom."

"Thanks, girlie." His eyes glistened. He glanced at his watch. "I better scoot. I've got some work to do at an old house across town. Think I'll tell the ol' girl good-bye before I leave."

Alone now, Ruthanne searched for Paul. She found him in the hospital lobby, sitting by the coffee kiosk. He had relaxed into a café chair, one leg crossed over the other. His hand rested on a round, white metal table and clutched the cardboard sleeve of a tall paper cup. His easygoing posture didn't fool her though. She could see the sadness in his eyes.

When he saw her coming, he quickly replaced the pensive look with a grin. "Hi, Ruthie. Coffee?"

The pungent aroma and a quick check of her stomach told her she couldn't handle anything stronger than tea. Her emotions had bounced her around worse than the river ride. She ordered green tea with a splash of lemon and sat at the table.

"You okay?" She tilted her head and prayed he'd share his feelings.

"Sure." He tapped the bottom of the cup on the table. "Just a lot to take in."

This corner of the hospital was quiet. Paul and Ruthanne talked together in relative privacy about how Hannie's illness had flushed out the pain in her life and brought her son back to her.

"Can you see that God was in it all, Paul?" She searched his face. When he finally dragged his gaze from the cup to her eyes, something different glimmered there.

"I can now. I'm sorry I couldn't have had more faith for you."

She grabbed his forearm. "Not for me. For you. You've been taking care of me—and Hannie—for too long. It's time you considered yourself." She stopped and then spoke her next words carefully. "I'll ask it again. Are *you* okay?"

He pressed his lips together and stared at his coffee. Finally a small grin bloomed on his face. "Yeah, I'm okay. I can see where all this played out for a reason. God knew what He was doing when He allowed Aunt Hannie to get sick. Even though I knew about the drug abuse, it was still hard listening to what her life was like before she met my uncle. But if she hadn't gone through it, she may never have developed the empathy she needed for her ministry."

"And what about your own mother? I'm sure this has dredged up some bad memories for you."

He took a sip of coffee and paused before answering. "I still have questions. But I'm learning that God is God, and He has a reason for everything He allows."

Skye came around the corner, and Paul greeted him with a broad smile. "Come join us. I was just getting ready to talk about you."

"Well then," Skye said as he perused the menu on the wall. "I'm glad I showed up." He ordered a cup of black coffee then pulled up an empty chair from the other table. "Tom is with my mother, so I thought I'd give them some private time." He sat and sipped carefully from the plastic lid. "So, I was about to be your topic of conversation?"

Paul leaned forward. "Ruthanne suggested the other day that she'd like you to learn the management side of the business. I know your time is up at the ranch, but if you still want to help, I can teach you to take over my duties."

Skye turned a warm blue gaze toward Ruthanne that made her toes curl. "I'd love to help out whenever I can on the ranch, and the computer work would be right up my alley."

Through the contented fog that had wrapped around her, Ruthanne finally realized what Paul was saying. Her heart cracked in two pieces. "You're not leaving, are you, Paul?"

"My grandmother called yesterday." Paul twirled the bottom of the empty cup on the table. "She says she's tired of keeping the restaurant going without my grandfather. Since he died a couple years ago, she's kept their dream going but realizes now that without him she'd rather move on."

Ruthanne swallowed. "Your grandmother lives in Crossroads Bay. That's on the coast."

"Same state. Only half a day away."

She ignored his flippant humor. "You're going to go and take over for her, aren't you?"

"Yes." He nodded. "I think I am." His eyes danced. "In fact, now that I've voiced it out loud, I'm kinda getting excited about it."

"Hey." Skye leaned forward in his chair. "Won't it be easier to start a catering business from your own restaurant?"

"That's what I'm thinking." Paul also leaned forward, and Ruthanne suddenly felt excluded. "It's already an established restaurant with a full staff. It couldn't be more perfect, really."

"Excuse me." Ruthanne had to be the voice of reason. Both men looked at her as if they'd just realized she was in the room. "What about the clientele you've already built up? And the investors you met with a week ago?"

"I got their call after my grandmother's. It's a no-go." Paul shook his head. "I think God is closing this door, knowing my grandmother needs me. Opening a window and all that."

Why did he have to take a leap of faith now? All this time she'd been trying to teach him this lesson, and he had to learn it when it would break her heart.

He stood and threw his cup away. "My grandmother gave me a couple of months to move down there." He shook Skye's hand. "Welcome aboard. Just let me know when you'd like to start." Then he slipped his hands into his pockets and whistled a tune as he left the hospital.

Ruthanne, suddenly aware that she was alone with Skye for the first time in several days, met his intense gaze. He cocked his head. "I'd say you look like you've just lost your best friend, but that wouldn't be funny right now, would it?"

"No." She sighed. "But maybe it's for the best. He sure looked excited, didn't he?"

"It's a good thing."

She nodded, feeling better as she began to see how Paul would benefit from this change.

"And now"—he brushed her thumb with his forefinger—"I want you to know what happened to me when I left a few days ago."

"Okay." He could tell her anything he wanted as long as he touched her like that.

"I prayed a foolish prayer the night I sat with my mother. I asked God for her to acknowledge me in some way. A happy grin, a glimmer in her eyes. . .something. When she just stared at me with no emotion at all, I had to leave. I was in so much pain." He lowered his voice as a customer came up to order an espresso. When he left, Skye recounted his time at the cabin.

"This morning I sat at the river, pouring my heart out to God. I started throwing rocks in the water and found with each effort I could release my anger." He rubbed his arm. He must have tossed quite a few issues into the river.

She smiled. "In the room it wasn't hard to tell that you'd found peace."

"I did, and to commemorate it, I made a rock altar on the riverbank." He pulled her hands up to his chin, and she thought he might kiss her fingers. "I want that peace for you, Ruthanne."

Even though his words thrilled her, they also caused a small pain in her chest. He was asking her to forgive Brian. She closed her eyes, not ready to commit fully to that. When she opened them again, he was still looking at her. As if to finalize his argument, he placed his next words on the table between them. "While searching the scriptures, particularly Mark 11:25, I learned that I couldn't ask God to forgive me until I had forgiven my mother."

In her silence, he released her hands. "I'm going to sit with my moth—my mom awhile longer." He stood and reached out to her. "Are you coming?"

જી

That evening as Ruthanne watered the alpacas, she thought about Skye's rock altar. Her garden hose could hardly compare to Skye's river, but the gentle lapping into the troughs, mixed with satiated alpaca noises, brought his words to mind.

She, too, needed to leave her burden on her Rock, Jesus Christ. For too many years she let her disappointing marriage color her decisions. The pain of knowing Brian never loved her and tossed her aside like one of his used painting rags still dug at her heart. But Skye had helped her to trust again, even though he tended to disappear. Knowing this was his coping mechanism—and that it was never permanent— helped to stretch her faith.

As was her custom, she visited Lirit last so she could linger with her into the evening. They nuzzled noses, and Ruthanne looked into the large perceptive eyes.

"I no longer want to hate Brian, Lirit. I'll never have the opportunity that Skye and Hannie had. I'll never be able to sit with him and hear how sorry he is or unburden myself of my own shortcomings during our marriage." Her voice caught as a small sob crept up her throat. "The past is over, and it's up to me to forgive."

Lirit's gentle hum reminded Ruthanne what it meant to be in God's will. She closed her eyes and placed her pain and disappointments on her Rock.

When she looked up, she saw Skye ambling toward the paddocks. A thrill shot through her. Was this confirmation or just a coincidence that he would be the first person she saw after releasing her anger?

&

Skye's lightened heart floated from his chest to hover around Ruthanne. Even in her dyed hemp "hippie" clothes, she never looked more beautiful.

He'd been so enraptured with her that he barely noticed the attention Lirit had decided to give him. But when he got to the gate, Lirit thrust her shaggy head into his vision and searched him with her pool-ball eyes.

Skye smiled at the gatekeeper and stroked her neck. "It's okay now, Lirit. With God's intervention, I'm worthy of her now."

Lirit blinked her long eyelashes, and even though her expression never changed, Skye knew she smiled. The alpaca pranced to a corner of the paddock and dropped to her knees, cushing in her contentment.

When he looked back at Ruthanne in the paddock, he noticed that his heart had not come back. It was waiting near her for his thoughts to catch up.

But unfinished business remained between them. He opened the gate and joined her. "I came over to tell you how sorry I am."

"For what?"

"For skipping out like that. It was rude to leave you worrying. I never wanted to hurt you."

"I'll admit that I was confused, but you didn't hurt me." She touched his arm. "Brian hurt me and made it difficult for me to trust another man. But you showed me what a real man is supposed to be."

He shook his head, not daring to believe her words. "As messed up as I was? I don't think I'm a great role model."

She placed her hands on her hips. "Listen to me. God used you to bring me to forgiveness." After the brief scolding, she reached up to entwine her arms around his neck, her gentle strength taking his breath away. "I'm at peace now."

He could see it. She no longer spat out Brian's name as if it were a disgusting bug caught in her throat.

"Well then, little lady." He suddenly felt playful as he adjusted his imaginary hat. "Think you can use another cowboy on your ranch?"

She tipped her head, teasing him with that delicious twinkle in her eyes. "That would be great if we had cows."

He reached around her waist and pulled her close. "I'll herd alpacas, chickens, and rabbits, just to be near you."

In the shadow of the giant sentinel, Singing Mountain, their lips met as she answered with a kiss. Above the joyful beating of his heart, he heard humming.

And if he could hear Lirit, he knew he was in God's will.

epilogue

Ruthanne looked out the french doors in the great room toward the north pasture where a small gathering of wedding guests awaited her arrival. They had chosen that part of the property for the grove of maple trees. It took on its role as wedding chapel without the benefit of ribbons, cut flowers, or candlesticks. Ruthanne reveled in the fact that God had painted her sanctuary with vivid purple lilacs and golden yellow forsythias. Their scents floated through the open french doors, reminding her of the day Skye had arrived at the ranch a year ago.

Her gaze drifted out the doors and to the guests. Her mother had just been seated. Up until a few months ago, they hadn't talked since she'd left with Brian. But once God healed her abandoned heart, she called her mom to start the healing process there. Hannie and Skye had inspired her.

Skye.

She imagined Tom, as his best man, giving him a pep talk in her mobile home. Tom had promised to keep an eye on Skye. "Wouldn't want him to run."

Ruthanne smiled to herself, unworried. Skye had promised never to run again.

She glanced around the large room. Hannie had surprised them at the wedding rehearsal, announcing that her present to the couple would be her house.

"It's way too big for me," she'd said, "and I've always loved that little mobile home. The house was a dream for David and me to share together. Now I rattle around in there by myself. I know he'd be pleased if you filled it with children."

Ruthanne's heart swelled with the thought of raising Skye's children in this beautiful place.

From the kitchen, she could hear Paul grumbling about something. She glanced at the clock above the fireplace. "It's almost time to walk," she called to him.

He mumbled then strode into the room.

"Are there problems with the food?" She laughed at his disheveled hair, knowing he had run his hand through it in frustration.

"No, the catering is going great. I just stepped into the office to see how Skye is doing with the inventory."

"Paul, it's been nearly a year since you've looked at that stuff. Do you have to do that today? Now?"

"I'm sorry, but I couldn't help myself. Skye has a different approach than I do. His logging system looks more like a real estate spreadsheet than a log of Hannie's creativity."

"Well, he knows more about houses than he does merchandise."

Paul finger combed his dark hair and adjusted his tie. "He's abbreviated every item. I don't know if AWS is alpaca wool socks or angora walking stick."

Ruthanne frowned. "Do we have an angora walking stick?"

"No. But that's not the point."

"Ah. He's messing with your system."

He stabbed the air. "That's the point."

The clock chimed two times. She glanced outside again, and soon Skye took his place next to their pastor. Even from this distance, he looked incredible in his white tuxedo and lavender shirt, a color she'd picked to make his blue eyes even more vibrant.

Paul held out his arm. "You ready?" She'd been married before, so she didn't feel the need for her father to give her away. But since she knew Paul would be hovering near the kitchen until the last moment, she asked if he'd at least walk with her to the back of the guests.

"I'm more than ready." She took his arm. "Thank you for coming back from the coast to cater and to escort me."

"You'd do the same for me." He stopped short, apparently realizing what he'd just said. "Except for the catering part. . . and the escorting part."

She squeezed his elbow. "I know what you mean. . .and yes, I would."

They walked together until they reached their destination, then he kissed her temple before taking his seat.

As Ruthanne prepared herself to lope—well, that's what she wanted to do—to glide down the grass-carpeted aisle, she was grateful she'd chosen a midlength dress, blue to match Skye's eyes. A traditional train would have come away with grass stains. She wanted an all-natural wedding, and it surprised her that Skye agreed.

Her feet pinched in the wedge sandals she'd chosen in lieu of high heels. She knew spikes would sink in the grass, and the wedge, the salesgirl told her, would look more fashionable than a normal sandal. But she longed for her rubber boots. She should have painted them white.

Hannie turned in her chair in the first row and beamed a huge grin. Ruthanne praised God for providing a mother-in-law she already loved.

The bridesmaid she had chosen made her laugh. Lirit wore a halter that was a piece of work in itself, with blue- and lilac-colored ribbons woven into a fluttering cascade that hung to her knobby knees. Tom had already led her down the aisle to the delight of all those watching.

Music swelled from the string quartet. To her immense surprise, rather than the soloist they'd lined up, Skye himself began to sing to her. Since forgiving his mother, Skye sang often. She'd hear him crooning to the alpacas while feeding them, or she would catch him humming in the office. Now his rich baritone voice assured her in melodious rhythm that God had created their union and nothing would be able to tear it asunder. The song drew her like a bee to a succulent flower until she found her place at his side.

He held out his hand to her. "Hello, my beautiful Calamity." His blue gaze warmed her until all she could think about was getting on with the ceremony to hasten the kiss.

But then her left toe started cramping. She tried to slip off the sandals discreetly, but Skye noticed, particularly when she lost two inches in the process.

He glanced down at her feet. "Comfortable?"

She grinned up at him. "I'm very comfortable, thank you, now that I'm with you." With a squeeze of his hand, they turned to the pastor.

The ceremony was brief, and finally Ruthanne kissed the man to whom she'd just pledged her life. As they stood in their forever moment, she smiled.

Was that Lirit. . .or was her heart singing?

Dear Reader,

Often authors are asked where they received inspiration for their story lines. The answers are as varied as the stories themselves. I'd like to share with you how this story came to be.

One day I was surfing the channels on television instead of writing. . .but we won't go there. . .when I found a show about people looking for lost family. A man in his forties had hired someone to look for his mother. She had been a drug addict, but obviously had other mental issues. She had kept her daughter, doting on her and denying his existence. I don't remember all the details, but I do remember his reaction. This was a near middle-aged man who turned into a child upon seeing his mother for the first time. It tugged at my heart enough to spark the idea laid out within these pages.

My character, Skye, is a man of God, but there is still one thing that keeps him immature. He hasn't forgiven his mother. Forgiveness is a biggie in the Bible. The lack of forgiveness causes stumbling blocks that we can't even see. Mark 11:25 couldn't put it plainer: "And when you stand praying, if you hold anything against anyone, forgive him, so that your Father in heaven may forgive you your sins."

I didn't start out writing a book about forgiveness. I usually get a spark of an idea and then let God take it from there. I pray if you identify with the issues within this story that you will release those rocks into the river and trust the Rock of your soul, Jesus, to lift that burden away.

Blessings,
Kathleen Kovach

A Letter To Our Readers

Dear Reader:
In order that we might better contribute to your reading enjoyment, we would appreciate your taking a few minutes to respond to the following questions. We welcome your comments and read each form and letter we receive. When completed, please return to the following:

Fiction Editor
Heartsong Presents
PO Box 719
Uhrichsville, Ohio 44683

1. Did you enjoy reading *God Gave the Song* by Kathleen E. Kovach?
   ❏ Very much! I would like to see more books by this author!
   ❏ Moderately. I would have enjoyed it more if

   _____

   _____

   _____

2. Are you a member of **Heartsong Presents**? ❏ Yes ❏ No
   If no, where did you purchase this book? _____

   _____

3. How would you rate, on a scale from 1 (poor) to 5 (superior), the cover design? _____

4. On a scale from 1 (poor) to 10 (superior), please rate the following elements.

   ____ Heroine   ____ Plot
   ____ Hero   ____ Inspirational theme
   ____ Setting   ____ Secondary characters

5. These characters were special because? _____
   _____
   _____

6. How has this book inspired your life? _____
   _____
   _____

7. What settings would you like to see covered in future
   Heartsong Presents books? _____
   _____
   _____

8. What are some inspirational themes you would like to see
   treated in future books? _____
   _____
   _____

9. Would you be interested in reading other **Heartsong
   Presents** titles? ❏ Yes   ❏ No

10. Please check your age range:
    ❏ Under 18   ❏ 18-24
    ❏ 25-34   ❏ 35-45
    ❏ 46-55   ❏ Over 55

Name _____
Occupation _____
Address _____
City, State, Zip _____
E-mail _____

HOOSIER CROSSROADS

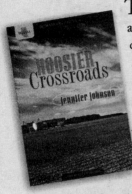

Three daughters of modern Indiana are in pursuit of fulfilling their dreams and finding peace. Kylie Andrews has risen from poverty, so she balks at Ryan Watkin's free-spirited approach to work and securing a future. Chloe Andrews is on the verge of graduating university as a star soccer player, until an injury benches her and Trevor Montgomery stand in the way of her goals. Lydia Hammond has failed at multiple jobs, but well-organized Gideon Andrews is drawn to her despite feeling obligated to another relationship. Can romance be the tool God uses to bring these women the desires of their hearts?

Please send me _____ copies of *Hoosier Crossroads*. I am enclosing $7.97 for each. (Please add $4.00 to cover postage and handling per order. OH add 7% tax. If outside the U.S. please call 740-922-7280 for shipping charges.)

Name_____

Address _____

City, State, Zip _____